THE SECRET OF
THE CRATER

THE SECRET OF THE CRATER

DUFFIELD OSBOURNE

THE SECRET OF THE CRATER

Published by Wildside Press LLC.
www.wildsidebooks.com

CONTENTS

THE SECRET OF THE CRATER

THE
SECRET OF THE CRATER

CHAPTER I

PROLOGUE

I WONDER how soon the time will come
when the world shall be so thoroughly
explored and its peoples so cosmopolitanised
that adventure and discovery will be things of
the past. A few days since I should have said
that this undesirable yet inevitable epoch was
already present with us; that the field of real
romance was even now synonymous with the
field of professed fiction. No more Odysseys;
no Circe; no Lotos-eaters; no more travels of
Sir John Mandeville; no Prester Johns, with
their mysterious courts. Even the wanderings

of Captain Cook had begun to read like the works of the modern story-tellers whose very inventions bade fair soon to reach a limit, and then the world would have nothing to do but settle down to the dead level of studying humdrum facts and pursuing material improvements.

From this well-nigh morbid condition I have been suddenly rescued, and in a way that brings most forcibly to my mind how much may be hidden under little. Who would imagine that a tale as wildly improbable as the wildest fictions of Verne and Haggard had lain for decades concealed under the formal phraseology of a dust-covered report in the naval archives at Washington, and that the key to its secret was in the memory of but one man, who has but lately gone forth to explore that country which alone must remain undiscoverable to the eye and mysterious to the prying intellect of flesh-encumbered humanity ?

I had been spending a few days in Washington, and, being invited to dine with an official of the Navy Department, I strolled around to his office late in the afternoon. I found him almost at his wits' end. One of the annoying incidents of bureau life had just occurred. The Secretary of the Navy had sent for a certain document, and it could not be found. Clerks scurried hither and thither, or stood around in awed and expectant silence. As I entered, my friend came forward.

" Will you pardon me if I keep you waiting for a short time ?" he said. " You see, in one of these general changes to which our political system is subject every four years, several filing-clerks have been dismissed, with the result that now and then some paper that's wanted might as well be at the bottom of the Red Sea. I don't believe the most perfectly devised system can entirely eliminate the personal element. Don't you want to come with me ? I'm going myself into one of the file-rooms, where it is just possible that what we're looking for may have been misplaced."

Having nothing else to do, I followed him. Then I heartily regretted my foolish complaisance. Dust rose in clouds, as bundle after bundle was drawn out, hastily examined, and thrust back again to accumulate a new coat. Coughing and half choked, I was about to excuse myself and retire, when, as a clerk dived into a new pigeon-hole, a grimy yellow document, unendorsed, fluttered to my feet. I picked it up gingerly.

" What 's that ? " said my friend, glancing hastily over my shoulder as I shook the paper open at arm's length. Then he added, in a tone of interest, " I 'll be hanged if it is n't the report of the loss of the *Falcon !* How the deuce did it ever get in here, and in that shape ? "

Taking it from me, he thrust it into his pocket, while I withdrew to the private office. He joined me there in half an hour, the dirtiest man I have ever seen outside of a coal-bin; but his search had been successful, and soap and water and clothes-brushes and clean linen were available. An hour later we sat down to dinner.

" Do you know," he remarked, suddenly, as we were sipping our coffee, " that paper you picked up was quite a find. Every now

and then some such document is seriously mislaid, and a record of the loss is handed down
from Secretary to Secretary, until most of
them that are not at once replaced turn up
sooner or later.   This," he continued, taking
it from his pocket, " has been missing since
1840, and we had entirely lost sight of the man
who made it.   Let me see."   And he opened
the pages and spread them out.   " Shall I
read it to you ?   It 's short, and rather enter-
taining."

" Certainly," I replied, not especially interested except in the satisfaction of my
friend.

He read as follows :

" BRITISH FRIGATE ' HALIDON,' AT SEA,
" February 8, 1839.

" SIR,—On the 7th of January last, Easter Island
bearing W.N.W., distant about ten leagues, the
United States sloop of war *Falcon*, Captain Nathaniel French commanding, met with a hurricane
which continued for two days with great violence,
driving us south and west.   Upon the storm abat-
ing, we found ourselves approximately in lat. 51°
20′ S., long. 65° 9′ W., being unable to determine more accurately on account of a deplorable

accident to First Lieutenant Hasbrook. This officer was washed overboard on the night of the 7th while attempting to take an observation with the only sextant we then had, and the instrument was thus lost.

" The sky clearing on the 9th, land was sighted upon the starboard quarter, two leagues distant, being an island about ten leagues in circumference, well wooded, and rising in the centre to a large cone-shaped mountain, evidently a volcano.

" No land appearing upon the chart at or near the point above indicated, Captain French determined to go ashore, and a landing was finally effected with much care and some difficulty.

" The island was found to be inhabited and fertile.

" We weighed anchor and sailed on the 16th of January, having experienced no further mishap except the loss of Second Lieutenant Vance, who was probably killed by the natives.

" On the 23rd of the same month, at about 5.40 o'clock A.M., while sailing E. by N. with a free breeze, the ship ran upon a sunken coral reef and became a total wreck. The boats were broken or upset, and all hands lost with the exception of myself. While swimming with the aid of a plank, I came upon a small boat bottom up, and, having succeeded in righting it, was rescued three days later by the British frigate *Halidon*, bound for Valparaiso.

" With this report I beg to tender my resignation
as surgeon in the United States Navy.
          " I have the honor to be, sir,
              " Very respectfully,
                  " Your obedient servant,
                      " BASTIEN DESHON, M.D.
" To Hon. Secretary of the Navy,
      Washington, D. C."

" That 's really a most curious production,"
said my friend, after a short pause. " The
writer does not seem to comprehend in the
least the true interest of his report. One
would think that the discovery of a new inhabited island would at least call for some
little specific information."

" What else do you know about it all ? " I
asked.

" Why," said he, " all that the Department
has ever known was that such a report was
received and almost immediately mislaid, and
that Dr. Deshon never reported in person or
by any further communication. There was
some tradition to the effect that the document
mentioned undiscovered land somewhere, and
officers cruising in the southern Pacific were
directed to look out for it; but nothing was

ever found, and I imagine they finally came
to the conclusion that hardships had unhinged
Deshon's mind.   He was a Louisianian, from
New Orleans, I think."

" Do you know how it strikes me ? " I said.

" No ; how ? "

" I think the whole narrative shows a deliberate intention to conceal the material facts."

" But why report at all, then ? "

" A sense of duty both to the government
and the relatives of the lost men ; the certainty
that knowledge of his rescue would come out
through his rescuers ; the chance of his arrest
as a deserter in case of his discovery and non-
resignation,—any of these ; probably a little of
each.   Then look at the report.   It is unendorsed, which at once gives it a good chance
to get mislaid ; it slurs over the most import-
ant features in a very marked way, and, to my
thinking, is purposely vague in fixing the loca-
tion of this island ; while it announces a great
discovery in words that are evidently intended
to indicate a very trivial one.   The most sur-
prising part of it all, though, is the off-hand
way in which it states that Lieutenant Vance

was ' probably killed by the natives.' Do you suppose for a moment that any commander of an American man-of-war would leave such a question unsettled, — would allow his first officer to be assassinated without visiting severe punishment on his murderers ? Then look at the surgeon's—to say the least—hasty resignation and non-appearance. Depend upon it, the whole thing is a careful attempt to conceal the facts and to avoid inquiry."

"It does look that way," said my friend, thoughtfully; "but what does the man want to hide ?"

"Ah! there you 've got me. Any one of a hundred things. I 'm going to try to find out which."

"You !—how ?"

"I 'm going to look up Dr. Deshon."

"Probably he 's been dead for years."

"More than likely; but all the same I 'm going to start for New Orleans to-morrow morning. It 's hard work for us poor novelists to find plots nowadays, and I can't afford to miss such a chance as this. Besides, I 'm really very much interested."

That was the gist of our conversation, and the following day, armed with such information about Dr. Deshon as the navy records furnished, I set out for New Orleans.

Fortune favoured me from the very first. At the only address which I had found in connection with his name—an old house in the most aristocratic part of the French quarter—resided a brother of the man I sought. This gentleman received me courteously but with considerable reserve. Still, by the exercise of some diplomacy, I learned that after Dr. Deshon had resigned from the navy he had spent many years in travel, much of it solitary and in out-of-the-way regions; that finally he had returned to his home; that he was now living, though upwards of eighty years of age, and resided part of the year with his brother, and the rest on a small plantation a short distance from the city.

Then, to cut a long story short, I arranged to meet him, which I succeeded in doing under very favourable conditions, was invited to visit him at his plantation, won his confidence by that simplest of all methods, proving that I deserved it, and learned from his lips the narrative which I am going to tell. You will readily understand that the object of the " years spent in travel in out-of-the-way regions " had been to rediscover the scene of his former adventure and to learn the fate of his friend, in both of which aims he had finally succeeded, and the only conditions he exacted were that I should not make the tale public until after his death and that, as a precautionary measure, I should not seek to locate the island any further than he had done. I have since found reasons to confirm me in my belief that the official report was not only vague but positively misleading as to this point. However that may be, I was pained to learn of the Doctor's death, which happened only a week after I left him; and you may believe me when I say that I would gladly have been compelled to withhold the story many years; for he was a charming gentleman, with all the frankness and hospitality of the old-school Southern planter grafted upon the tact, wit, and pleasing manners of his French ancestors.

CHAPTER II

LAND!

IT was the morning of the 9th of January, 1839. The hurricane, which for two days had driven the *Falcon* before it, abated almost as rapidly as it had commenced its revels, and the sun poured down upon the ocean, whose bosom still heaved with memories of the agitating breath of her tempestuous wooer. It was with considerable anxiety that land had been sighted a quarter of an hour before. Now, however, the feeling was quite different, as officers and men gazed out upon a richly wooded island, with the crater of a huge volcano rising up in its centre like the boss of an ancient shield. Buildings, low, but of considerable extent and built of a white material, peeped here and there from among the trees.

Naturally the ship's company were deeply

excited. A new island! a new people! It was with difficulty that, beating in as near as they dared, they curbed their impatience until the swell should subside sufficiently to permit of a landing being effected.

It soon became evident that the presence of the *Falcon* was the occasion of no less interest upon the shore. Crowds could be seen assembling on the beach and hurrying hither and thither,—men with dusky faces and wearing rough tunics of some dark material, while here and there among them were others with long white tunics and red cloaks. These latter seemed to be of a lighter complexion. Certainly they were in authority, for they carried short whips, with which they struck such of the rabble as pushed forward too roughly.

Soon, however, the attention of the Americans was distracted from the scene upon the beach. An exclamation from one of the sailors turned all eyes to where he pointed, and a boat, half galley, half canoe, was seen gliding out from behind a headland. Propelled by ten rowers, it swept toward the man-of-war. In the stern sat one of the red-mantled men like those noticed among the crowd. The oarsmen were dark, almost black, and naked but for short aprons that hung from their girdles.

Certainly the purpose of these visitors did not seem hostile, and Captain French made ready to receive them with all the ceremony he could muster, barring a salute which he forbore firing for fear of its terrifying effect upon men probably unused to gunpowder. Nearer they came. Their craft, with its prow carved to the semblance of some animal's head, suggested in a measure those galleys of the ancients that were known as " Liburnians." Now the rowers had brought her alongside, holding themselves well off with their great sweeps until a receding wave allowed them to glide near enough for him of the red cloak to grasp the companion-ladder and mount to the deck.

He was a tall man, of lithe, athletic build, with complexion almost as light as a Spaniard's and features like those of an Arab, while the thick, closely curling black beard added an even more Semitic character to his piercing dark eyes and prominent nose. His demeanour was entirely fearless and composed. His dress was as I have described it,—a white, sleeveless tunic reaching almost to the feet and confined at the waist with a belt in which was thrust a short sword with a serpentine blade, somewhat like a Malay kris. A mantle, bright red in colour, hung gracefully from his shoulders over bare, muscular arms, and his costume was completed with buskins fastened about the ankle with crossed thongs.

The crew of the *Falcon* had been piped to quarters while Captain French and Lieutenant Vance stepped forward to greet the stranger. The latter stood with arms crossed upon his breast and bowed very low, though with considerable dignity. Then he spoke slowly, pointing from time to time toward the shore. The language was entirely unlike any of the South Sea dialects, and such of the officers and men as were versed in tongues, civilised or barbarian, were summoned forward, but without avail.

Again the man endeavoured to make his meaning understood, and this time an expression of deep surprise came over the first officer's face. He suddenly became closely attentive. Then he essayed to answer, in hesitating and uncertain accents, at which the other smiled indulgently. Nevertheless, much to the surprise of all, he seemed to grasp the sense of the American's reply.

Lieutenant Richard Vance was known throughout the service as a man of very studious habits, with a pronounced *penchant* for Orientalism. He was an excellent Hebrew scholar, and some of his fellow-officers even averred that he could speak ancient Egyptian. Be that as it might, he certainly was able to communicate, in a fashion, with his ship's guest.

After a few minutes of conversation, voluble on one side and halting on the other, Vance turned toward the Captain and said, with a puzzled expression:

" Perhaps you will laugh at me, but, unless I am strangely mistaken, this chap has been talking very decent Phœnician or Punic. I 've rummaged a little in both, as far as a man can nowadays, and I 'm pretty well up in Hebrew,

which is practically a dialect of Phœnician or
vice versa,—God only knows which.   The drift
of it all is that he bids us welcome to the land
of somebody named Merrak, and wishes to
know whence we come, that he may make a
report to his master.   I 've told him as well as
I am able."

" Ask him if we can find a safe anchorage
closer inshore," said the Captain.

" Would you follow his piloting ?   It would
afford an excellent chance for treachery," suggested Vance.

"Ask the question," said the Captain, curtly.

Vance flushed, and, turning to the other,
spoke at some length.   Finally, with the aid
of considerable gesticulation, his meaning was
made plain.   The islander replied that there
was deep water and good bottom around the
headland whence his boat had come, and that
he would consider it an honour to pilot the
Falcon to a safe and convenient harbour.

The offer was promptly accepted.   Addressing a few words to his boat's crew, he intimated
that, if the ship would follow in their wake, it
would find what was sought.

2

The anchor was thereupon weighed, and, with only her foresails set, the *Falcon* began to glide through the water churned into white foam by the strokes of the brawny oarsmen ahead. The stranger made no effort to leave the man-of-war's decks, and her officials were thus relieved from any necessity of openly detaining him as a hostage for the good faith and knowledge of his followers. He continued, however, to direct the course of the latter from time to time by shouted commands.

Vance leaned over the bow and observed the rowers. They were men of a type not especially different from other races of the Pacific, and unquestionably owned no racial kinship whatever with their commander. The mind of the Lieutenant was busily employed trying to frame some theory which would explain the presence of such a man in such a place.

Richard Vance, executive officer of the *Falcon* since the death of Lieutenant Hasbrook, was in his thirty-first year, of middle height, and of a build calculated more for endurance than for any great muscular effort. His features would have been called strong rather than handsome, though grey-blue eyes, light brown hair that waved about his temples, and a drooping blond moustache went to make up a personality which was decidedly pleasing — to all but his commander.

Captain Nathaniel French was something of a martinet; an excellent officer, as the phrase goes; quick in action, and of undoubted courage. He lacked, however, all those finer attributes of the man that win and retain respect or affection. His manners were rough, and he scoffed at education beyond what might be necessary to make a report, keep accounts, and navigate his ship. Therefore it was not strange that he had never regarded with favour a student like Vance, whose greatest failing was that he saw too much of both sides of a question to let him take either with the best effect; and that gentleman's becoming first officer by the death of his superior had not served to soften the Captain's dislike. Then, too, the sudden and unquestionable benefit to be derived in the present emergency from Vance's learning was regarded by Captain French very much as a direct and rather impertinent reflection on his own well-known views on such subjects.

Still the dark-bearded stranger stood with folded arms near the bowsprit. From time to time his eyes wandered over the ship and crew with an expression of curiosity and interest he could not wholly suppress. It was evident to all that this man was, to say the least, a very superior type of savage. All surmises, however, in this or other directions were abruptly broken off; for, as the *Falcon* rounded the headland, the curving shore of a well indented harbour came into view. Here, sheltered from winds and waves, a dozen or more galleys, several of them of considerable size, rode at anchor or were drawn up on the beach. No houses appeared near the water, but some distance back, upon rising ground and between the landing and the great mountain crest, the astonished eyes of the Americans made out what seemed to be a city of considerable extent and possessing no little claim to architectural beauty. Many of the buildings were lofty and most of them, together with the walls, a long stretch of which was clearly distinguishable flanked at regular intervals with high towers, were built of some white material that glittered in the sunlight like marble, adding a brilliance to the general effect, though it seriously interfered with much detailed scrutiny.

The ship had approached to within perhaps half a mile of the bay's head when the pilot turned to Vance and indicated that they should come to anchor. The necessary orders were promptly given and obeyed. Everything had taken place so rapidly that even the power to wonder had been in a measure suspended. Now, however, at the Captain's suggestion, Vance approached the man and requested that he would partake of some refreshment.

Bowing again very low, the latter replied that this was impossible; that there was one higher in authority to whom it was his duty to make an immediate report of the result of his visit, and whose pleasure he must learn with reference to the strangers.

Then, summoning his crew, he descended into the boat, and their long sweeps bore him rapidly toward the shore.

CHAPTER III

MERRAK

NOON came, and still there was no sign of movement upon the land. The galley had been drawn up on the beach, and the chief and his men had disappeared in the thick jungle that came down almost to the water's edge. Captain French began to grow impatient.

"Mr. Vance," he said suddenly, as he ceased pacing up and down the deck and drew his watch from his fob, "if something does n't develop within the next hour I shall not delay going ashore."

Vance bowed.

"What are your views?" he continued.

"I have no very definite views on the subject," replied the Lieutenant, a little stiffly; "but I hardly think I should force matters, under the circumstances."

" No, I don't suppose you would. That 's
where we differ. You booky men would never
accomplish anything. You 'd spend all your
time thinking it over and reasoning out your
course, and when you 'd made up your minds
what to do, it would n't make much difference
what you did."

Evidently pleased with this shot, he turned
on his heel and continued his walk, glancing at
his watch from time to time as the sun began
its downward course.

Vance's first impulse was to imprecate his
commander in good Anglo-Saxon; his second
to do it in bad Punic; and his third, to laugh.
He compromised the matter by smiling,—
perhaps the most irritating comment of all.

Just what Captain French would really have
done never transpired, for suddenly the many
eyes that had been spying out every foot of
the shore-line, from the moment the ship had
anchored, saw a strange procession issue from
the woods. First came a confused and jostling
crowd of the dark-skinned natives; then a
company of perhaps fifty of the lighter race,
clothed in their long white tunics and bearing

round bucklers and drawn swords with serpentine blades. Closely following these and
surrounded by other guards similarly dressed
and armed, a gorgeous litter was borne out
upon the sand, while behind it, bringing up
the rear of the strange procession, walked
eleven men, ten of them marching two and
two, and the eleventh at their head. These
latter, though evidently of the darker race,
seemed, from their rich garments, to occupy a
station not inferior to that of their lighter
companions. They wore red tunics similar to
the white ones of the others, and black mantles instead of red ones hung from their
shoulders.

There was little if any confusion or delay in
the movements of the entire concourse. The
litter was set down, and a tall, black-bearded
man stepped from it. All prostrated themselves before him. Then, accompanied by the
armed men, who appeared to be his guards,
and followed by those with the black mantles,
he advanced to the water's edge and entered
one of the small galleys, several of which were
swiftly launched and rowed toward a great

galley that, with a horse's head carved at the prow and twenty long oars thrusting out from either side like the legs of a centipede, rose and fell lazily about a cable's length from the shore. Quickly, and still with perfect order and decorum, the crowd mounted to her deck, he who was evidently their king or chief taking his place under a broad canopy that covered the high poop. The anchor was then raised, the oars swung to and fro, timed by the measured strokes of a mallet wielded by a man who stood at the prow, and, thus propelled, the vessel, with her sharp projecting beak parting the ripples like the blade of a cutlass, bore down upon the *Falcon*. Several of the latter's men fixed their eyes rather nervously on this dangerous ram and stole hasty glances at Captain French, who stood quietly upon his quarter-deck and awaited developments with apparently perfect confidence in the amicable intentions of the new-comers.

As the strange craft approached nearer she sheered gracefully off, her starboard oars were quickly withdrawn through their port-holes and she was brought alongside the ship with

an ease and accuracy of handling which no
ordinary skill and training could have attained.
Then, while some of the crews of both vessels
employed themselves with fenders of rope or
logs in keeping their sides from grinding
against each other, a narrow gangway which
had been raised upright against a stout post
set at the bow of the galley—a contrivance
strikingly similar to the ancient boarding-
bridges used with such effect by the Romans
—was let down upon the *Falcon's* deck, binding the two firmly together.

All hands had been piped to quarters to receive the august guest, who now arose from his
couch beneath the awning and, supported by
two of his chiefs, crossed the bridge fearlessly.
He was a large man, perhaps fifty-five years of
age, and inclined to corpulence. His complexion was a deep olive, his beard black and
curling, while upon his strong and rather
haughty features was an expression of such
profound weariness or depression that it might
almost have been called despair. His dress
was like that of the chief who had first visited
the ship, except that his red mantle was deeply

embroidered with saffron, and around his brows ran a slender gold circlet.

With a careless glance at surroundings which could hardly have failed to excite in him a very lively curiosity, he approached Captain French. That commander bowed in greeting, but the other, without making any answering obeisance, spoke several words in a voice that contained the same suggestion of mingled pride and sadness which his face seemed to indicate.

The Captain turned helplessly to Vance.

" He merely says that you are welcome," interpreted the Lieutenant.

Meanwhile many of the escort of the island potentate had followed him aboard,—perhaps half of those who seemed to be his guards,— while the rest stood drawn up on the deck of the galley. The dark-faced men with red tunics and black cloaks had also crossed the bridgeway. Viewed closely, they were un- questionably of the same Polynesian race as the oarsmen and the rabble; but the sparse beards were shaven from their faces and the coarse black hair from their heads, while around the smooth brows of each ran a narrow band of gold from the front of which rose an ornament of the same metal, which seemed made in imitation of a jet of flame. The fillet of one, a very corpulent man well advanced in years, with features that bore evidence, so far as features can, of a nature both cruel and crafty, was decorated with three of these golden flames.

"I say, Mr. Vance," whispered a young midshipman, irreverently nudging the executive officer in the back, "what 'll you bet the dark gentry are n't clergymen ? See how the black-bearded fellows make way for them and stand around and look respectful."

"But not very affectionate," replied Vance over his shoulder, for Midshipman Price was a favoured individual on the *Falcon*.

Both remarks seemed not unwarranted. More than one of the officers were quick to note something peculiar in the relations existing between these representatives of two races, distinct and yet dwelling together upon an island hitherto cut off from the rest of the world. That the chief and those around him feared and showed marked deference to the others was perfectly apparent; that they nevertheless looked down upon them, in a manner, as inferiors, was almost equally clear. What in the men with lighter skins seemed the haughtiness born of a conscious superiority that owed some allegiance which it could not break, was met by these members of a priestly caste (for Price was evidently correct in his surmise) with a suggestion of the insolence usually shown by inferiors who have in some manner laid their masters under subjection. Vance remarked all this very rapidly, as the priests, with the unrestrained curiosity of savages, passed hither and thither about the ship, handling everything within reach and casting none too friendly eyes upon such of the crew as fell in their way. As for their leader, him of the three flames, there were at once tacitly established between himself and the Lieutenant those unaccountably hostile relations which the first interchange of glances often carries between utter strangers.

Meanwhile, the chief, with such of his followers as he selected, including the priests, was escorted into the cabin and entertained with all the form and courtesy which the navy regulations prescribed.

Through Vance a fairly intelligible conversation was possible, and the islander plied his entertainers with questions as to their own country and the causes which brought the ship to the neighbourhood of his island. All these were answered as fully as Vance's vocabulary would permit, and the answers were received with close attention but in a manner which gave no indication as to how they were regarded. The priests, too, listened attentively, and from time to time addressed remarks to each other in a strange and barbarous but unquestionably Polynesian dialect which was unfamiliar to all the *Falcon's* officers.

When, however, Vance, at the instance of Captain French, sought to question their guest in turn, he answered shortly and in a manner indicating that he held it his province to ask rather than to reply. This much, however, was learned:

The island was called by its inhabitants Karana and was governed by himself, Merrak,

under the title of Soveet.   The white race to
which he belonged considered themselves the
nobility or ruling caste.   Their ancestors had
sailed thither from far over the sea many ages
since and had gradually, by reason of their
superior knowledge and civilisation, gained an
ascendancy over the native race which had
previously been very savage and primitive.
Yes, the dark men with the flaming fillets were
priests.   They were of the aboriginal stock,
because the strangers had adopted the religion
of the island; and on all theological matters
these priests were very learned and held
supreme sway.

Finally the Soveet, having eaten and drunk
sparingly, signed to his followers to rise, and
all ascended to the deck, where he made his
farewells with the same reserve and dignity he
had preserved throughout.   Turning to Vance,
he said :

" Tell your master to come to my city to-
morrow when the sun has reached half-way to
the mid-sky, that I and my people may welcome you all."   After a short pause, he added :
" My servant Esbal—he who first greeted you

—shall attend at the shore with a suitable escort, to look for your coming."

Without waiting for an acceptance of this command rather than invitation, he passed over into the galley. She pushed off; the oars rose and fell again to the rhythmic strokes of the mallet; the small boats relieved her of her company, as they had brought it to her, and the whole concourse vanished silently into the woods.

That night Dr. Deshon slipped into Vance's stateroom for a smoke before retiring. The latter was deep in his books, and the surgeon puffed for a while at his cigar in silence. At last, unable to restrain his impatience longer, he said:

" What do you make of all this business ? "

Vance closed the book. " I don't make very much of it yet. Events have followed so quickly on each other that they are all more or less mixed in my mind. As for conclusions, they are almost impossible."

" Have n't you an idea about these people? "

Vance smoked thoughtfully with knitted brows.

" I suppose I have a theory," he said at last. The Doctor nodded, and he went on. " The language they speak is unquestionably a dialect of the Phœnician tongue, about which we don't know much except that it was n't very different from Hebrew. Fortunately, I happen to understand Hebrew pretty well. I could get the sense of about everything the Soveet said and could make some sort of fist at talking back. By the by, did you notice his title ? It 's very suggestive of the old Carthaginian ' Suffet '; and the names Merrak and Esbal — especially the latter — are almost pure Phœnician or Punic. The horse-head prow to the galley is significant too. It was the favourite Carthaginian device, you know."

" Then you think—— " said Deshon.

" I know this much," pursued Vance, leaning forward: " that the Phœnicians, and after them the Carthaginians, were the maritime people of the ancient world; that there are records to the effect that they sailed through the Straits of Gibraltar, down the coast of Africa, and perhaps around the Cape of Good Hope. Of course it 's a good way from there

3

to here, but I really don't see why it 's impossible, and no other supposition will explain what we have seen and heard to-day. The more I think of it, the more I feel like qualifying what I just said, — that I had come to no conclusion. I have about come to a conclusion that these men are the descendants of some ship-load of Carthaginian exiles who were driven out in one of the faction fights so common in that city, and that, somehow or other, they were blown south-west around Cape Horn. You see, they must have had their women with them, for it is quite evident that those we saw to-day have kept their stock clear from any native intermixture. As for the natives, the Soveet explained their presence and position naturally, if it needed any explanation."

" Well," laughed Deshon, " it looks very much, after all, as if you know all about it. You 're too modest, my boy."

" I 'll tell you what bothers me, though," said Vance, ignoring the last remark; " and that is, the position and evident power of those priests. How did the inferior native race come to give its religion to the others ?   From what I saw of its ministers, it is n't a religion of love by a long shot.   You can be sure that there 's a very lively conflict going on here between Church and State, with plenty of hard feeling thrown in."

" Then they really must have reached an exceptionally high plane of civilisation," said the surgeon, laughing.

" Yes, but—— "

" You don't mean to tell me you expect to solve that, too, to-night ?   I never thought you were so conceited.   Why, you have n't a scrap of data; and, moreover, I, as your physician, forbid it.   For the general good, I 'll allow you to puzzle over your Hebrew or Phœnician or whatever it is, for one hour longer, and then you must turn in."

Vance smiled.   Deshon snapped his cigar-stump through the port-hole, nodded to the Lieutenant, and returned to his own stateroom.

CHAPTER IV

KARANA

MORNING came. No sooner had the first shades of grey heralded the sun's advance up the ocean, than all hands on the *Falcon* were awake and stirring. Both officers and men had too much upon their minds to sleep well, while Vance's appearance made it evident that he had lengthened the hour of study which the Doctor had allowed him until its measure was the night itself.

There was little preparation to be made for the visit to the shore, so the men had nothing to do but wait with such patience as they could command. Curiously enough, there seemed to be no fear of treachery from the islanders and no hesitation about trusting themselves among vastly superior numbers of a people about whom little or nothing was known.

Nearly a third of the ship's company were detailed to remain aboard, much to their own disgust, and the shore party were to go fully armed; but, beyond these very obvious measures, no precautions whatever were taken. Probably Captain French relied, in case of attack, on the effect of their firearms, the operation of which he had ordered to be carefully kept secret. Certainly no advice was offered him by anyone after the curt manner in which he had received Vance's former suggestion of prudence.

As for that officer, it is probable that the Captain's dislike would have relegated him to ship duty for the day, but the importance of the only man who could communicate with their hosts was too compelling to admit of such treatment; so the *Falcon* was left in charge of one of the midshipmen, and the boat's crews gave way for the beach almost as soon as Esbal and the escort were seen issuing from among the trees.

Soon the keel grated upon the sand. As the men hurriedly disembarked, twenty black-beards, as Midshipman Price irreverently termed them, with their round bucklers and serpent-blade swords, came forward and made obeisance. In a few words Esbal indicated that he would lead the way, and that his men would deploy at intervals on either side of their visitors, in order to keep the rabble from pressing upon them: so, in this order, the march commenced.

A path, narrow and evenly paved with hexagonal blocks of lava, wound westward through the forest. Four men only could walk abreast, and the long column of one hundred and fifty of the officers and crew of the sloop of war, two and two, between their silent guides, pushed on, nervously conscious of the ease with which an ambuscade could assail their straggling array. It was with a feeling of sincere relief that Vance and Deshon saw the underbrush disappear and the trees thin out into what might be called a well-kept grove.

Then suddenly a spectacle burst upon their sight that caused them to halt in amazement. A broad plain, thronged with a motley multitude and dotted here and there with white villas of considerable extent, stretched away

to the same brilliant city they had observed
from shipboard, but grander and more beautiful a thousandfold at this nearer view. The
scene was one of veritable enchantment that
wanted nothing but a few rocs and flying
horses and genii-shaped clouds to make the
beholders believe they had awakened on an
Arabian Night, whence the slave of the lamp
would shortly issue to perform their pleasure.

Not less than fifteen thousand men and
women, all in holiday attire, crowded both
sides of the path, which broadened out into
an avenue as it drew clear of the woods. A
single glance at this vast gathering, weapon-
less and crowned with garlands, showed two
things: first, its entirely amicable spirit, and
second, the probable uselessness of resistance
should treachery be intended. The march
was resumed in a more condensed column, and
men and women—the latter being all of the
darker, native type — swarmed around the
foreigners, gazing upon them with curious but
not unfriendly eyes and striving to touch their
persons or weapons whenever the whips of the
escort were not to be feared. Very few of the

ruling race, who seemed to occupy the position of both a military caste and a nobility, were in the crowd, and these evidently for the sole purpose of maintaining due order and decorum.

The city itself was now hardly half a mile distant. As they drew nearer, the walls were seen to be built, not of marble, but of great blocks of coral or some coral-like rock. It mounted in successive terraces along the gradually rising ground, and was evidently of even greater extent than the sea-view had given promise of. The gates were open, and Esbal, passing through, led the way up a broad, well-paved street. At this point the common people were left behind as though forbidden entrance, but the house-tops were thronged with the bearded nobles, while here and there could be seen the unmistakable flutter of female garments. Flowers, too, began to fall upon the procession, as it pressed on, more slowly, perhaps, as anxiety and distrust gave way to livelier curiosity.

Then came the grand *dénouement* of the march. A sudden turn of the way brought the head of the column upon a spacious public square surrounded by buildings of much greater pretensions than those that bordered the streets. Porticos of white coral pillars formed their façades, fountains were playing here and there, while at the farther end of this magnificent plaza rose flight upon flight of steps that extended its entire width, leading up to a broad platform upon which stood what was evidently the palace of the Soveet himself. In front of this building a brilliant assemblage was gathered. At least two thousand armed guards surrounded the canopied throne whereon sat Merrak, while a company of young girls, perhaps fifty in number, clustered behind it and viewed the new-comers with a curiosity which had in it much of welcome.

Dark spots, however, were not lacking to the festival array. On either side of the throne and beyond the circle of the guards were drawn up dense bodies of priests, also armed with swords. Their black mantles served to cast a shadow over the rest of the concourse, and in their faces was nothing of the welcome that beamed elsewhere. At one corner of the square rose the windowless walls of a great tower-like structure, evidently of some military strength and built entirely of blocks of lava — a gloomy fortress amid the houses and palaces of white coral that glittered on every side. A second glance showed that its summit was thronged with priests.

" I say," whispered Midshipman Price to Deshon, " there 's the temple of these fellows' god, whoever he is. I 'll bet he 's a pretty grim sort of deity."

" He must be an improvement on Moloch with his human sacrifices," said Vance. " I hardly wonder that our Carthaginian friends, if that 's what they are, thought nearly anything would be a beneficial change. But wait a bit; I 'm going to try a little scheme of my own, later on."

Further conversation was stopped, for now the Soveet rose from his throne and, descending, embraced Captain French with every sign of welcome.

" I hope the court ladies will adopt that style of greeting," remarked Price, in a remarkably resonant whisper. The Captain glanced back and frowned, while Vance, stepping forward at the same moment, said:

" Soveet of Carthhadtha, we place ourselves as guests in your hands."

A look of intense surprise flashed across the calm face of the other. Then, composing himself with an effort, he replied:

" Young man, you speak words that may mean much, for you name the name that tradition says was borne by the birthplace of my race."

The eyes of Vance were radiant with triumph as he communicated his words and the reply to the group of astonished officers. Then he turned again to the Soveet.

" To my nation," he said, " much is known. It was not difficult to divine the origin of the men who govern this island which you call Karana."

The potentate, who had now regained all his dignity, bowed in acquiescence with the explanation.

" Let your people enter my house," he said, " and they shall receive such hospitality as we can offer."

So saying, he led the way within, under the portico, through a broad hallway, and out into an open court evenly paved, and with fountains playing at the four corners. Here were many tables piled with an Oriental profusion of fruits and other edibles, while women of the darker race were busied drawing from great sacks a thick syrup-like liquor which they mixed with water and poured into cups of metal ranged along the boards. Long benches were provided for the accommodation of the guests, and officers and sailors made short delay in partaking of this unusual feast; the former being seated apart near a couch whereon the Soveet reclined at the farthest side of the court. Priests and nobles occupied many of the tables. All men drink in the same language, and under the warming influence of the liquor—rather a sweet, heavy cordial than a wine or spirit—tongues were loosened, reserve was in a measure thrown aside, and the men of the *Falcon* soon became friendly with their hosts, or at least with the Karanian nobles.

Around the court on every side were galleries

with little curtains fluttering between slender pillars, and behind these it was evident that the ladies of the Soveet's household were watching the festivities. Dark eyes could be seen peering curiously here and there between the hangings, and now and then the pretty ripple of suppressed laughter was borne down to the ears of the feasters below. Glances, too, were from time to time cast upward, but evidently these beauties preferred or were obliged to be very chary of their charms.

Suddenly Vance clutched Dr. Deshon's arm tightly. The latter started. " What 's the matter ? " he said. The Lieutenant did not answer for a moment. He was looking fixedly up at the gallery directly above the Soveet's couch, and the surgeon, following the eyes of his friend, was almost startled into a like unconsciousness of all around them.

Between two curtains that were held apart by hands as small as those of a child but having all the slender delicacy of a woman's, they saw a face so beautiful that no man could see it and look aside. Of a delicate tea-rose tint, flushing warmer where the blood rose in the cheeks, with long Oriental eyes that seemed to draw their light from some fountain of liquid fire far behind them, a broad low brow clouded with a mass of hair black as night, and a mouth for which Gabriel might have joined the hosts of Satan, — it was no wonder that Vance and Deshon could only sit and gaze speechless.   But there was a charm about the face that was more than that of mere feature. An expression of indescribable sadness lay in the eyes, and the mouth seemed almost about to utter a supplication.   It suggested vaguely to Deshon the look that the face of the Soveet wore, but in a woman, and a beautiful one, it roused very different feelings, and seemed to call out every chivalrous impulse that a man's nature could comprehend.

It was evident that her action had been entirely unconscious, for suddenly she seemed to realise that the eyes of Vance were almost burning into her own.   Drawn down as if by some irresistible impulse, her gaze fell and, for a moment, she looked straight at him. The colour slowly deepened in her cheeks; then they paled, and Deshon could plainly see the effort with which she stepped back and allowed the curtains to drop together.

When the surgeon turned toward his companion he was almost frightened at his face. It was white as the coral of the table before him, and his look was still fixed rigidly upon the swaying curtains.

" Come," said Deshon, sharply, " you 'll attract attention. Your friend the high-priest, or whatever he is, is looking at you."

Vance recovered himself with an effort. " Did you ever see anything half so beautiful ? " he said slowly.

" Frankly, I don't believe I ever did," replied the Doctor; " but all the same you must n't get yourself and perhaps all of us in trouble by any inadvertent captivation. You know the most marked difference between barbaric and savage peoples is that the former are usually very jealous of their females; and these fellows are pretty well up in the barbaric scale."

" Deshon," said Vance, " I 'm going to marry that woman."

" Nonsense! You 're crazy," exclaimed the surgeon.

" I know it," said Vance. " I always told you I was a fool about some things; but I think you 'll admit that even French could n't growl at me on the score of indecision—— "

" I say, Mr. Vance," came the voice of the Captain from farther up the table, " you 're not doing your duty as the only man who can keep up our end of the conversation. Ask the old Soveet—or whatever you call him—whether that volcano up there is in working order or has gone permanently out of business."

Vance put the question mechanically, but the effect produced was startling in the extreme. The face of the Soveet grew pale, and, rising hastily from his couch, he crossed his arms upon his bosom and bowed low toward the mountain's crest, above which hung a film of mist or vapour. Such of the nobles as caught the tenor of Vance's question and all who saw the action of their ruler, immediately prostrated themselves upon the ground. The priests alone remained seated. A hurried whisper seemed to pass among them and their frowning brows met the astonished eyes of the *Falcon's* officers wherever they turned to seek some explanation of the disturbance.

At length he whose fillet bore the three flames stood up and, stretching his hands toward the mountain, seemed to address it. He spoke in what was evidently the aboriginal dialect. Then he turned and spread his arms over the prostrate Karanians, speaking again in a low, deep voice. His face had become absolutely expressionless. Suddenly he ceased, and the people rose slowly to their feet.

After this strange incident, Captain French noticed a certain constraint in the manner of his entertainers and, deeming it best to resume relations at some more propitious season, he took an early opportunity to bid the Soveet adieu and give the orders to return on shipboard. It was none too soon, for the day had passed quickly, and the sun was well down toward the horizon when the man-o'-war's-men issued from the palace.

Since he had caught a glimpse of the beautiful Karanian, Vance had been like a man in a dream; and now, as he descended the long sweep of the steps, his abstraction seemed to bear fruit. His foot slipped at the lowest step and he fell heavily to the pavement. Dr. Deshon was at his side in a moment, as the Lieutenant raised himself on one knee.

" Not hurt, are you ? " he asked.

" I 'm afraid I am—a little," said Vance, with a grimace of pain.

" Where ? " queried the surgeon.

" My ankle," replied Vance. " Easy there ! don't wrench it," he added, as Deshon proceeded to make a hasty examination.

" Nothing broken," he said, at last, " and I don't find any swelling. See if you can't get up."

Vance tried to stand, but immediately sank back again with a groan. The Soveet and those of his suite who were nearest appeared deeply concerned and were profuse in their offers of aid.

" I think you had better leave me here for the night," suggested the Lieutenant. " It 's late. There's no sense in my hampering your march, and you can send a hammock for me in the morning. The old fellow here says he 'll take care of me."

Deshon looked hard at the injured man. Then he leaned over and said, in a voice too low for the rest of the officers to hear:

"Dick Vance, you 're no more hurt than I am. It 's all put on, and that woman 's at the bottom of it. For God's sake, don't be a fool."

"Don't speak so loud," the other whispered. "I *must* stay here for the night. There are one or two things I 'm bound to get to the bottom of. I 'll promise to be careful, though, Doc. Don't you worry, old man," he continued, as the surgeon hesitated. "I 'm old enough to look out for myself, and there is n't a bit of danger."

"I 'm not so sure of that," muttered Deshon, again appearing to examine the injured ankle.

"Well, I don't care if there is, then; and, besides, I 've got to live up to my new character for decision."

"What 's the matter?" exclaimed Captain French, bustling up. Word of the accident had recalled him from the head of the column.

"I 'm afraid," said the surgeon, slowly,

'' that we shall have to leave Lieutenant Vance here until we can send a hammock for him in the morning. His ankle appears to be— sprained — or strained ; and these people say they are ready to take care of him. I shall stay, of course, too.''

Captain French frowned. "Can't he walk?'' he asked.

'' No,'' replied Vance, quickly, before the surgeon had time to answer.

The Captain hesitated a moment, deeply annoyed.

'' Well,'' he said finally, '' we certainly can't all spend the night here, and if Mr. Vance has got to stay, I suppose he must. I won't run the risk of leaving you, though, Doctor. He'll have to take his chances,—that's all. Fall in there, men.''

Deshon looked troubled, but he had allowed himself to go too far for withdrawal and he knew the hopelessness of remonstrating.

Reluctantly he retired with the others, but, glancing back as they entered the street, he saw two of the islanders lift his friend up and carry him back into the palace.

CHAPTER V

ZELKAH

THE Lieutenant found himself domiciled in a small room opening off one of the galleries that surrounded the court of the Soveet's house. His apartment was fitted up with considerable taste, not to say luxury. The small couch was covered with a velvet-like cloth dyed red. Hangings of the same colour draped the walls, and mats were spread upon the floor. There were no windows, and ventilation was had through a row of small square apertures near the ceiling, which could not be closed except by a short curtain running upon a rod. A metal lamp in the corner shed a soft, rich light over everything.

Scarcely had Vance been placed upon the couch by his bearers, when the Soveet himself, attended by several nobles and a single priest, entered.

" I have brought to you one of our physicians," explained his host, at the same time indicating the priestly visitor. " He is skilful, and will examine and attend to your hurt."

" I cannot thank you enough," replied Vance, with some embarrassment, which he found it impossible altogether to conceal. He felt that the eyes of the priest were reading him and that he must get rid of that individual's services or run a very serious risk of his ruse been exposed.

" Surely you will understand me," he went on, after a moment's hesitation, " when I say that we are accustomed only to the methods of treatment of our own physicians. Besides, I do not think the hurt is at all serious," he added, noticing the expression of surprise that crossed the Soveet's face. " I shall be all right in a day or so; in fact, the pain is less now. Rest will be all it needs and I shall not ask you for more than this and a little food."

" As you wish," replied the other, in impassive tones. " My women shall attend you and provide for your wants."

He turned and passed out with his attendants, the priest-physician being the last to
leave.

As the latter disappeared, he cast at Vance
a look which certainly was not altogether
friendly, and which made the American con-
gratulate himself with considerable fervour
that he was out of such hands, at whatever
cost. His reflections, however, were by no
means complimentary to his tact.

" I 'm making a fearful mess of it," he
pondered. " I wonder how many of these
people suspect me. I should think they all
would." Then he tried to fix his mind calmly
upon the events of the last two days, with all
their wonderful import. What a crazy scheme
this last one of his was! What could it possibly accomplish ? What did he want to accomplish ?

His meditations were interrupted by a soft
footfall in the corridor without. Then a
woman's voice asked if its owner might serve
the stranger with food and drink. Vance's
heart bounded at the accents, only to subside
as rapidly a moment later when, before he had

composed himself sufficiently to answer, two girls entered the room.

They were undeniably pretty, but not with the beauty of which he dreamed, and he watched them as they drew a small table near his couch and spread out upon it a repast of fruits, goat's milk, bread and a sort of cheese-cake. She who had spoken did not address him again, probably presuming, from his failure to answer before, that he was ignorant of their speech, but from time to time both glanced at the invalid with eyes wherein curiosity and interest were mingled with shy-ness. At last the younger spoke to her companion in a low tone:

"This cannot be the stranger whom you imagined our mistress was pleased to observe. That was the one who interpreted for them, and this man did not understand my words."

"Very possibly it is not," replied the other, shortly, "but such things are not for you to chatter about."

One idea after another thronged through the Lieutenant's brain. These girls would soon be gone. He must arrange to see his lady of the balcony, if only for a few moments; and yet, could he trust them ? Would not even a disclosure of the fact that he understood their language be of disadvantage, after they had spoken as freely as they had ?

" You had better straighten out that cloth," said the older girl of the two. " The Lady Zelkah will perhaps come to see if we have served him well, and you will be punished."

Vance felt his face flush and grow pale again. She was coming—coming to visit him. He should see her again and speak with her. At that moment, as if to make the words good, a rustle of garments sounded from the corridor, and the veritable princess of his dreams stood before him in the doorway. A white tunic with open sleeves, belted at the waist with a gold cincture and fastened here and there with curious jewels, fell to her feet, while a long mantle suspended from brooches at the shoulders and caught again at the waist hung in graceful folds about her. Her face was even more beautiful than when Vance had seen it through the curtains. After a moment's hesitation, she stepped forward into the room.

The maids, together with two others who had accompanied her, stood with bowed heads and arms crossed upon their bosoms.

As for the American, from the moment she had entered, his eyes were powerless to look aside; but the girl did not seem to notice the intensity of his gaze. She approached the couch and met his glance with one in which sympathy and interest were blended with a childish frankness.

" Are you hurt much ?   Have you been well attended ? " she inquired.

Vance's resolution was quickly taken.

" I am not hurt at all," he replied, in a low whisper. " I wanted to see you again. Will you forgive me for telling the truth ? "

She shrank back.   Fortunately none of the maids could have caught his words, but the two who had spoken so freely could see that he had answered their mistress, and were at once plunged into evident confusion and de-spair at the recollection of their indiscretion. Vance felt that he must disarm any possible enmity on their part, and he added:

" I have been better cared for than I could

dare ask, and your maids are as kind as they are beautiful."

She was now meeting his look with an expression of deep and serious thought, while the colour bloomed and faded and bloomed again in her cheeks. Then, with a little air of imperiousness mingled with embarrassment, she turned to the attendants.

" Withdraw to my apartments and await me there," she said.

The women bent their heads and retired, not without their faces indicating some surprise. When they had gone, their mistress came close to Vance and asked:

" Why did you wish to see me ? "

If he had ever harboured an instant's doubt as to his feelings, it had been dispelled long since. Time and words were very precious and risks were not to be considered.

" Because I love you," he replied.

Again she drew back with a startled look.

"Oh, no, no!" she murmured. " That is impossible. You do not understand. You cannot."

Vance had risen from the couch, heedless of

the danger of interruption. He came up to her and took her hands.

" What is impossible ? and why may I not love you ? " he said. " You are not one that it is hard to love, and surely you are the wife of no man ? "

She shook her head, and an expression almost of horror came into her eyes.

" Do you not know that I am the Soveet's daughter ? " she replied.

Vance was troubled by her words, although he had already felt certain as to her identity and had discounted it in his calculations. It could hardly fail to make success more diffi-cult, but the thought of ultimate failure was one that he had firmly put out of his mind from the first.

" I know I am very presumptuous," he said; " but I love you, and your father will give you to me. I am not without rank in my own country—a country so vast that many thou-sands of islands like this could be compassed within its boundaries and where the tide of men and women in a hundred cities streams back and forth like foam-flecks in the surf."

It is an old saying, and one about which
there can be no manner of doubt, that lan-
guages should always be taught by pretty
women who can understand no tongue but the
one to be learned. Vance felt that he could
have talked on forever in this strain. The
halting words halted no longer; but the expression which came slowly over her face
checked his speech as with a sudden chill. It
was the same look of inexplicable sadness that
he had seen through the curtains of the gallery.
She made a gesture with her head as if begging
him to be silent; then, drawing her hands
from his where they had rested in seeming unconsciousness, she stepped back. He found
himself seized by a premonition of evil, such
as sometimes descends on men's hearts to warn
them of approaching disaster. Twice she tried
to speak, and her words came at last with an
unnatural force.

" Do not dream of such things," she said.
" I tell you, what you talk of is impossible,—
utterly."

Then he began to realise how absurdly sudden his declaration had been.

" Do not misunderstand me," he pleaded.
" I should not have spoken to you as I did.   I
cannot hope that there should be now in your
heart any such love as is in mine; but, remember, I remained only to see you and I knew if
this opportunity were lost I might never win
another.   Forgive me for startling you with
so sudden a suit, will you not ?   I felt that I
must tell you."

The slender frame of the girl seemed agitated
by some deep emotion.

" Listen to me, of whatever race you be,"
she said, " that you may know that it is not
surprise or foolish bashfulness that restrains
me—that I can be as frank as yourself when
my heart demands it.   I, Zelkah, the daughter
of Merrak the Soveet love you; and yet I
say you must put me from your soul.   There
are reasons which I cannot even name that
would make your suit your ruin."

As she spoke, Vance had stepped toward
her, and now he drew her close to him.

" Do you think for a moment," he said,
" that people who love give up those they
love and who love them, because of a little

danger ? I shall take you to our ship, and
there is no power upon this island which can
wrest you from me.''

A noise in the gallery without came to their
ears. She raised her arms and, drawing his
head down quickly, kissed him. Then she
sprang away.

" You must never think again of what has
happened to-day,'' she said, in a low, sad
monotone.

She was gone, and the next moment the
form of the physician-priest darkened the doorway. The man's face wore a sardonic smile
when he saw the invalid standing erect in the
middle of the room, but his voice was super-
ciliously soft and deferential as he said:

" I was bidden by the Soveet to visit you
again, but I see your foot has already no need
of my care. I will report to him that you are
improved.''

As he turned to go, Vance stepped forward,
barely remembering to limp painfully. He
felt a strong impulse to strike his unwelcome
visitor to the ground, hasten after Zelkah and
compel her to accompany him to the shore;

but the absurdity of such a mad course was too apparent for even a lover to harbour the thought long.

"You will tell the Soveet, also," he said, savagely, "that I desire an audience of him in the morning—at daybreak, if he will."

The priest bent his head, still with the same disquieting smile of mingled cunning and malice, and withdrew, while Vance, again unmindful of his pretended hurt, fell to pacing the narrow room. Sleep, however much needed, seemed impossible, and then, too, he felt that there were influences at work which might make it imprudent to resign himself to a single moment of oblivion. It was almost morning before Nature irresistibly asserted her rights, and his eyes closed for a short hour's preparation for what he had determined should be a day of battle against the fates that opposed him.

CHAPTER VI

AROO

SUDDENLY he awoke with a start. The grey light of morning was stealing into his room, and by his couch, looking down at him, he saw the smiling face of the same priest. He was conscious of a shock to his nerves in realising how completely he had been in the power of a man whom he felt to be his enemy. The afterthought was, however, more composing. He was safe. Therefore it seemed evident that assassination was not a danger to be anticipated.

" It is morning," said his awakener. " The Soveet will receive you; and, if you can walk readily, I will lead you to him."

Vance could not detect the least tinge of sarcasm in the tone.

" Or would you eat, first ? " continued the other.

5

" No," said Vance, decidedly. " If you will lend me your shoulder to rest upon, I think I can go with you, and I prefer to go at once."

No further words were spoken, and the Lieutenant, having hastily made himself as presentable as possible, limped slowly out, leaning upon the arm of his guide.

The galleries, corridors, and halls through which they passed seemed interminable, but at last they reached and entered a small chamber. The Soveet was seated upon a curiously carved chair with curving feet, on either side of which stood one of his nobles. Vance glanced hastily at his face, to divine, if possible, whether he had been inspired with any suspicions, but it wore only the expression of passive, hopeless melancholy which he had before remarked.

In a few words Merrak questioned his guest as to his injury and expressed a courteous pleasure to learn of its improvement. Then came an embarrassing silence.

" Grant me," said Vance at last, nerving himself for his course, " that I may speak with you in private. There are things I wish to say which it may be well that no other should hear.''

The Soveet looked fixedly at the young officer for a moment, and, turning to his attendants and to the priest, made a sign that they should withdraw. Then he bent his eyes again upon his guest, and said:

'' Speak now.''

The American's words came to him halting and uncertain, but he gained in self-control and fluency as he felt himself launched upon the struggle which must make or mar his life.

'' Is it contrary to your law,'' he asked, '' that your daughters should wed with strangers ? ''

'' No such question has ever come before us,'' replied the Soveet, slowly. '' We have long been a people dwelling apart and knowing nothing of men beyond, except by the old traditions. Nevertheless, I see no reason why such marriages should not be.''

'' Then hear me,'' cried Vance, eagerly. '' It is I who ask to marry one of your maidens.

I am rich. In my country there are no kings
or soveets or nobles, but each man is a ruler
to himself under the law. To such a land I
would take her of whom I speak, and I can
offer much to recompense her for the rank
and pre-eminence she may surrender. It
is—— ''

Vance hesitated, doubtful how to disclose
the identity of the object of his suit. The
Soveet raised his hand.

" It is not necessary that you should say
more," he said. " All that has happened has
come to my ears. I know who it is that you
seek and I know what you have done that
you might speak with her. It is even possible
that your fair face may have won favour in her
sight, nor do I altogether condemn you, for I
know that it is the part of youth to be rash
and heedless in such matters. But listen now
to my words. What you ask is utterly beyond the power of man to grant—even beyond
mine, who am Soveet of all this land and its
peoples. Though my heart were with your
desire, yet it would be hopeless. Let this
matter be to you, then, as a dream which has

passed before your closed eyes, for no more
than this can it ever be.''

Vance stood silent and dumfounded at this
disclosure of Merrak's knowledge of all his acts
and motives. There was something, too, in
the ruler's voice that seemed despairingly decisive. The latter looked pityingly at the
young man.

'' Do not think,'' he resumed, in a gentle
tone, '' that I am hostile to you or your
people, or even that I do not recognise certain
advantages that might come to me from such
a marriage as you propose. You are doubtless
more powerful than we in many ways; but there
is a power nearer at hand which overmasters
any inclination I might have in your favour.''

A feeling of mingled determination and re-
volt had gathered strength in Vance's breast
as the Soveet spoke, and, when the latter had
concluded, he burst out:

'' Whatever the powers may be that oppose
what I desire, let me have but your consent to
contend against them. My people do not fear
shadows, and I even accept your words as an
omen of success.''

Merrak seemed to ponder deeply. It was evident that he was labouring under strong agitation. At last he said:

" I do not wish you to doubt my friendliness nor my will to serve you. It is therefore my wish that you should see how powerless I am."

Rising, he struck a gong that hung over his seat, and immediately one of the nobles presented himself, bowed low, and stood with folded arms awaiting his master's orders.

" Beg the Lord Aroo, the favourite son of Tao, to grant me his presence on a matter of most serious import."

The noble bowed again and disappeared, while Merrak sat with chin buried in his robe.

After a few moments, that seemed an age to Vance, he saw the heavy curtains that veiled all the sides of the room agitated near the Soveet's chair. Then they parted, though there had been no sign of a doorway observable at that point, and the figure of Aroo, the high-priest, stood in the aperture. The deep red of his long sleeveless gown seemed in malignant contrast to the black of his cloak, while the triple flames upon his fillet gleamed with a fire

as baleful as that which lay in his black, bead-
like eyes. As his glance stole from the Soveet
to the American and rested at last upon the
former, Vance felt more strongly than ever
that he was in the presence of a bitter enemy.

Rousing himself from his gloomy revery,
Merrak communicated to the priest in a few
words the nature of the stranger's request.
The face of the listener lost nothing of its im-
passiveness and inscrutability during the recital.

" And you have answered ? " he asked,
when Merrak had finished.

" Nay, I have summoned you that you
might answer."

" The Soveet honours too much the servant
of Tao," replied the priest. " Were there,
then, no laws that might have guided him in
replying to such a question ? "

The lines of trouble deepened upon Merrak's
brow.

" The case was novel," he replied, in a timid
and hesitating manner.

" But is not the law ancient and immov-
able ? " said the other, quickly. Then he came
closer, and, speaking in the native dialect,

seemed to reproach and, at times, almost to threaten; while the Soveet sank back trembling in his chair and made a motion as if to cover his face.

Vance viewed the strange spectacle with mingled feelings, among which astonishment and indignation predominated.

" You refuse my suit, then ? " he said sternly to the priest, when the latter had turned from the stricken ruler.

" I refuse not that which it is not in my power either to grant or to refuse," was the reply.

" But you have advised your master to refuse ? "

" I have advised the *Soveet*," replied the priest, raising his head and meeting the angry eyes of the American with a look serpent-like in its steadiness, " that he obey the laws, so that the god of the land shall not destroy him and his people. Least of all would I favour a stranger whose course has been one of duplic-ity, from the feigning of injury to the violation of hospitality toward the daughter of his host."

Vance made a step toward his accuser.

Then he checked himself, remembering his surroundings and the madness of attempting to resent the priest's words. The latter had put up his hand as if to command silence, and he now continued with dignity:

" Know, too, that the daughters of our soveets are reserved for a higher destiny than to become the brides of wandering foreigners who choose to admire them; a destiny noble in its office and glorious in its reward. It is Aroo, the favourite son of Tao, that has spoken in defence of his father's rights and in behalf of a people exposed, even by this moment of their ruler's weakness, to just wrath."

The Soveet uttered an exclamation of horror and pleading, and Vance glanced quickly toward his shrinking figure. When he turned again the priest had gone, and only the agitation of the hangings indicated the place of his exit.

" How dared that man —— ? " began the American, hotly, but the other checked him with pale face and trembling lips.

"Utter no evil of the lord Aroo," he said

hurriedly, while his eye sought the still swaying curtains in evident terror.

" Surely you do not fear him—you, the ruler
of this island ? " cried Vance, a strain of contempt mingling with the surprise that rang in
his voice.

" You do not know—you cannot know or
dream," replied the Soveet, struggling to regain his composure. " Therefore do not talk
of what you know not, or think to contend
against a power that is too strong for you and
even for me."

" Too strong for you it may be," said the
American, carried away by the force of his
feelings but speaking very slowly and deliberately. " Whether it be too strong for me, I
shall take occasion to make trial."

He checked himself, realising at once that
he had said too much; but the Soveet, far
from being offended at his guest's words,
seemed even to regard him more favourably,
and a gleam of something almost like hope
lighted up his sad face. Whatever might
have followed was, however, cut off by the
return of the same noble who had gone to

summon Aroo into the royal presence. He came to announce that men from the great ship had arrived to take the stranger back to his friends.

Vance hesitated a moment. There seemed to be nothing more for him to do now, and he felt, too, that whatever he attempted in his present excited condition would be as apt to work injury as good. There was, above all, the need of time to think over and weigh what had happened and to lay his plans and obtain such assistance as he might require to carry them out. Certainly the girl could not be in any immediate danger, although the vague fate that hung like a cloud over her own and her father's happiness must be one of more than usual horror. A life of enforced religious seclusion — the explanation he had first grasped at — seemed entirely disproportionate to the deep-settled melancholy inspired. True, these people were in a measure barbarous—especially the priesthood; and yet it would be insanity to act now upon any of the surmises that came thronging to him unsought and made his blood run cold. He must have time to think.

Turning, therefore, to the man, he signified that he would accompany him. Then, having made his formal acknowledgments and adieus to the Soveet, who seemed almost unconscious of his speech and presence, he passed out of the room, leaning upon the arm of the messenger.

As they crossed the great court, Vance could not restrain his eyes from roaming over the galleries to seek some sign of Zelkah's presence; but the curtains hung motionless, and the entire building seemed devoid of life or movement.

Before the palace, they found six sailors provided with a hammock, but the Lieutenant put it aside on the plea that his ankle was much improved, and, taking the arms of two of the men, he walked back through the city and along the path to the shore, whence a waiting boat soon conveyed him to where the *Falcon* lay swinging lazily at her anchorage.

CHAPTER VII

CAPTAIN FRENCH

CAPTAIN FRENCH stood upon the quarter-deck and watched his executive officer being assisted up the side. Vance promptly limped forward and reported for duty.

" How 's your foot ? " asked the Captain. " I see you favour it a bit yet. Better see Deshon about it."

" I think I 'm practically all right," replied Vance. " It does n't bother me much now."

" Well, no doubt you 're the best judge," said French, turning away.

Vance hesitated. Had he not realised that the Captain was no friend of his, he would have been strongly tempted to make a confidant of him, at least to a considerable degree. Even as it was, he considered that it would be just as well to know at once how much aid he might expect from that quarter.

" Pardon me, Captain French," he began.

The latter turned.

" There is a matter concerning which I should like to have a few words with you — in your cabin, if you are disengaged."

The Captain eyed him sharply for a moment.

" Certainly, Mr. Vance," he said.   " If you will come with me now, I shall be glad to listen to you."

He led the way below, and the Lieutenant followed.   Soon they were seated in the Cap-tain's room.

" Well," said the latter, pushing a decanter of whiskey toward his visitor, " help yourself, and let 's hear what you have to say."

Evidently Captain French was in a good humour, and Vance launched out into his narrative.   He detailed rather fully but guardedly the facts which had led him to the conclusion that the daughter of the Soveet was in danger from some form of fanatic influence, taking especial care to suppress all that bore upon his personal interest in her welfare.   Whatever else the Captain might be, he was not a suspicious man and, where another might have surmised or probed for a motive in his Lieutenant's action, he simply took the story as it was told him and, upon its conclusion, went straight to the practical side of it all, with the question:

" Well, what do you want me to do ? "

" It seems to me that we should take measures that will prevent any harm from coming to the woman, and, if necessary, carry her away on the *Falcon.*"

The Captain bit the end off a cigar, lit it, puffed once or twice, and replied:

" I can't say that I see it in just that light, Mr. Vance."

" Do you mean to say that you do not conceive it your duty to prevent an act of barbarism which may result in the death of a woman of rank ? "

" Look here, now, Mr. Vance," said French, taking the cigar from his mouth; " I don't know what 's started you on this ultra-humanitarian tack, but I 'll tell you how it strikes me. In the first place, you have n't a single scrap of evidence that these people intend to injure the girl. All it amounts to is that she and her father seem blue and appear to be under the thumb of a priest who has some plans for her future. Perhaps she 's engaged to marry him; perhaps she 's vowed to some kind of a South Sea nunnery. These people are not savages, and her father is their ruler. Is it natural, under the circumstances, to jump at such a far-fetched conclusion as you have ? Frankly, if I should proceed to kidnap the daughter of the ruler of even a semi-civilised state on any such flimsy ground as this,—or, for that matter, on any ground at all, — it strikes me I should be a very promising subject for a court-martial.''

Vance was silent. It was impossible for him to blind himself to the common sense of the Captain's views, and yet he was not prepared to yield to them.

" Well, sir,'' he said at last, '' is there any objection to our requiring some sort of guarantee that no harm is intended to the girl ? ''

" Oh, certainly not, certainly not. By all means go at once to the old chief and politely

ask him if he is going to cut his favourite
daughter's throat and have her served up at
lunch to the high-priest and his friends.
Seriously, though, Mr. Vance, does n't it
occur to you that you are making something
of a fool of yourself ?   Excuse me for expressing myself quite so plainly.   I don't mean to
cast any general reflection upon you, but only
upon your action in this particular instance.''

The Captain rose and knocked the ashes from
his cigar rather impatiently.   Vance coloured
and rose also.   He was angry and disappointed,
and yet he could not but recognise the im-
pregnability of his superior's position.   It was
evident that, unless he had something new to
advance, the interview was over, and he fully
realised that to disclose his true position would
be only to suggest to the other an apparent
motive for his request, and that motive the
desire to kidnap a young woman for entirely
selfish reasons.   Therefore he merely bowed
as composedly as he could and prepared to
withdraw.

" I may as well say, too," continued the
Captain, as Vance stood with his hand upon

6

the door, " that my orders and the delay occasioned by this storm make it necessary to get away from here as soon as possible. I expect to sail some time to-morrow afternoon and our time would be altogether too short for any such investigation as you propose, even were it practicable or could it lead to any allowable interference."

" Do you mean to say," said Vance warmly, " that if you knew my fears were justified you would still refuse to act ? "

" I mean to say," replied French, " that, while I don't cross bridges until I reach them, I am inclined to think that I could not see my way clear to interfering."

" And we sail to-morrow ? ".

" Such is my intention."

Lieutenant Vance went to his stateroom. He threw himself down in his bunk and tried to think. At first all his ideas were confused by the rapidity of their sequence, but gradually the situation began to shape itself in his mind.

That he was deeply in love, for the first time in his life, was the all-pervading thought.

That the object of his love was exposed to
serious danger of some vague and mysterious
character, he was unable to doubt, though he
could not but admit that the tangible evidence
would fit either of the Captain's suppositions
almost as well as his own. Still, he felt that
he was right, and he had considerable confidence in his intuitions. Thirdly, he saw
clearly that, whatever might be threatened, he
could look for no help from any armed intervention on the part of his ship, and that even
any intervention on his own part must be made
effectual during the next twenty-four hours.
Then the horrible consciousness of his utter
helplessness in the face of an insupportable
calamity came over him, and he writhed under
the torture.

Suddenly he sat up. What was he thinking
about ? Had he admitted to himself for a
moment the possibility of abandoning her ?
Let the ship go! he would remain and fight
it out. Then followed another revulsion of
feeling. To remain meant desertion, the worst
disgrace that could befall a soldier, and, if captured, court-martial and severe punishment.

Yes, but the disgrace of it! That was the real obstacle. Still, it was not like desertion in the face of an enemy. The ship and the service would get along just as well without him. There would be a scandal, and some good fellow, probably a more efficient officer than himself, would receive a well-earned promotion. A new idea flashed through his mind and he sprang up joyfully. Certainly it was practicable. Even the disgrace need not be inevitable. No one but Dr. Deshon would be sure that he had deserted, and the Doctor was his friend and would hold his tongue. Vance began pacing his narrow quarters. The thought of the helplessness of a man, alone and among a hostile nation, to contend against the danger he feared, hardly occurred to him. All he considered now was how to be able to throw himself into the scale, and he began to see a path to the accomplishment of this end. He pushed open the door of his stateroom and made his way to the quarter-deck. Captain French was still there alone, and Vance approached and saluted.

"May I ask, sir," he said casually, "when

you expect to go ashore again ? I presume
some such formality will have to be gone
through before sailing."

"I don't think it will be necessary for me
to go in person," replied the Captain. "I
shall probably send you with a file of marines
to make my excuses and farewells."

Vance struggled to control the expression of
exultation which he felt rushing to his face.

"That is," continued French, "if you have
gotten over your curious delusion and think
you can refrain from embroiling us with these
people."

The Lieutenant smiled. He was too well
pleased with the turn affairs had taken to
resent any remarks that were not absolutely
insulting.

"When shall I go, sir ?" he asked.

"As early as possible in the morning," replied the other. "I shall weigh anchor at
noon, or as soon as you can come aboard."

He turned aside to give some order, and
Vance hurried back to his stateroom and pro-
ceeded to lay his plans for the next day.
First he took out and carefully examined his

pistols, a very handsome brace of the newly invented Colt revolvers presented to him by Dr. Deshon. Then he packed away about his person as much ammunition as he could carry, and made a foray upon the steward's room, returning with a small bag of ship's biscuit. Finally, having filled his largest flask with brandy, he turned in for the night and slept as sleeps a man whose mind is undisturbed by the petty problems and uncertainties that are always so much more annoying than the really great troubles we know to be inevitable.

CHAPTER VIII

DESERTION

THE morning dawned cloudy and threatening, but Vance appeared on deck at an
early hour. A boat was promptly lowered and
manned, and half a dozen marines tumbled
aboard. Then the Lieutenant, having received
his parting instructions from Captain French,
went over the side, and, bowing rather ab-
sently in reply to a last admonition to make as
much haste as he found practicable, ordered
the sailors to give way for the beach.

They were soon ashore, and, leaving the
boat in charge of the bluejackets, Vance and
the marines commenced their march toward
the city. The way was unencumbered by the
crowds of the previous day; the party was
small, and moved quickly. Here and there
they encountered one or more natives of the

aboriginal race, who were apparently early risers, but they had almost reached the gate before the country seemed entirely awake.

An audience with the Soveet was obtained, and Vance performed his duties in truly diplomatic fashion. He represented how that Captain French's orders made his early departure an unfortunate necessity, in view of the delays occasioned by the storm; he made the excuses of his commander for not bidding their host adieu in person, and ended with the customary expressions of good feeling, to which was added their gratification at having been the first of the outside world to come in contact with a people so intelligent and friendly as the Karanians.

The satisfaction and regrets of the Soveet followed in due form. Not a word was said on either side as to the interview of the preceding day; and at last, amid many mutual assurances of regard, final leave was taken, and the Lieutenant and his men set out upon their return journey, attended by an escort of Karanian nobles.

They had nearly reached the beach. The

probability of an accompanying escort and the presence of a crowd of islanders curious to get a last look at the strangers had, oddly enough, not entered into Vance's plans. However, there was no time to be lost. Suddenly he halted his party with an expression of deep annoyance, paced backward and forward several times and finally, calling the sergeant of marines, gave him briefly to understand that he had neglected a matter which must be attended to before leaving. It would not, however, be necessary for all to go back; he would return alone, while the sergeant should lead the men on to the landing and wait for him there.

They parted, and Vance hurried back along the path.

It seemed as if no turn of the way would take him out of sight of groups of natives who were hastening to the shore, but at last the opportune moment came. For an instant he found himself free from the prying glances of curious eyes, and he grasped it to turn aside and plunge quickly into the thicket.

Fortunately, the undergrowth, while dense

enough to conceal him, was yet not of a character to seriously impede a man's progress, and he pushed on as rapidly as due exercise of caution allowed. Now and again he halted and listened. The chattering of many voices had died away in the distance, and the gathering of the people along the path and at the landing, while it had impeded the inception of his escape, seemed now to be turned into a favourable element of the situation.

His idea had been to get as close as possible to that edge of the cover nearest the city,—a position whence he could see best what was going on with the least risk of being seen,—and then to work his way around until he reached the heights beyond. From that point his way would be comparatively clear to the great forest-clad mountain, among whose ravines a safe hiding-place might readily be found until search should be given up.

From the moment the plan occurred to him in his stateroom, Vance had reasoned that the course he was now following would clear his name from the stigma of desertion. Captain French and Dr. Deshon might suspect him, but even Deshon could not be absolutely certain; while the mass of the ship's company and his friends at home would rest assured that he had either met with foul play from the natives or had wandered away and been lost in the wilderness of a strange region. So, reviewing the situation with some complacency, and smiling at the thought that he had not even had to lie to the sergeant of marines, he at last found himself in that part of the island which lay beyond and above the city. The sun was already well up, and as yet there was no sign of suspicion visible either along the shore or on the *Falcon* which he could now make out riding easily at anchor but showing the unmistakable symptoms of a man-of-war about to put to sea. With a parting glance he turned again and plunged farther westward into the ever-thickening depths of the forest.

During the earlier part of his flight frequent villas and cultivated clearings had rendered détours necessary, but now the farther he advanced the wilder and more unfrequented became his surroundings, until at last all signs of the presence of man disappeared.

While congratulating himself on this, and beginning for the first time to feel that his escape was made good, he came suddenly upon a small path, well kept, but so narrow as to admit the passage of but a single individual. It led straight on toward the mountain, and the fugitive, after a quick calculation to the effect that by following it he would travel more rapidly and easily and would leave less of a trail, made his determination accordingly. Then, too, he realised that a man moving carefully along a beaten track would make much less noise, and be thus more likely to detect the presence of another before he could be himself discovered.

He had not, however, gone far before an increasing light among the branches ahead warned him to be cautious, and a moment later he found himself peering out into a small circular clearing from which every tree and stump and bush had been scrupulously removed. The ground was covered with a growth of soft grass, cut close and showing every sign of constant care and attention.

All this was disturbing enough, but the

building which stood in the centre of the area
filled the fugitive with much more serious concern.   It was an odd-looking structure, circular in shape and, as he roughly calculated,
about twenty feet in diameter and fifteen in
height.   The material was an almost black
stone which seemed to be profusely ornamented with fantastic designs cut in bas-relief,
conspicuous among which were semblances of
jets of flame.   No window, door, or aperture
of any kind appeared upon the side nearest
him, but a narrow winding stairway curled
around the circumference and led up to a
gently sloping roof with a platform in the
centre.

Despite the manifest imprudence of such an
attempt, Vance felt himself irresistibly drawn
to make some closer investigation of the building.   Perhaps an undefined idea of its possible
availability as a readily defensible stronghold
lurked in a mind that had been devoted to the
study of military matters, but all that he was
conscious of was an overmastering interest and
curiosity.

In pursuance of this impulse, he first care-

fully circled the clearing, under cover of the
bushes, and satisfied himself that there was no
break in the wall.   Evidently the edifice was
not intended as a place of residence.   Then
suddenly it flashed across his mind that it
probably had some connection with the religion
of the island: a temple, most likely; for it
was built of the same material and ornamented
with the same designs as the great temple that
flanked the palace on the city square.   Upon
this supposition he reasoned that it was unin-
habited, but, to make sure, he threw several
small stones at the wall, in order to lead any
possible occupant to disclose himself.   In such
event he trusted to the woods for concealment.

No evidence of human presence, however,
followed his demonstration, and, reassured, he
hurried out into the clearing and proceeded
to climb the stairs.   In a moment he was
upon the roof, which he noticed was also made
of blocks of stone, sloping somewhat toward
the raised platform in the centre where yawned
a circular orifice about two feet in diameter.
Drawing himself cautiously up to this, Vance

peered down into the dark interior. The odour of heavy perfumes came to him with an almost stifling strength. Gradually his eyes became accustomed to the blackness. He leaned farther over, and at length began to be able to distinguish objects below.

The interior of the walls was decorated with fantastic flame patterns tinted in red, yellow, and black, intricately combined and composing into what seemed to him like weird faces looking up from the gloom. The floor was covered with carpets of skins. A richly canopied bed of some yellow metal, possibly gold, stood at one side, while tables, couches, and chairs of a similar material, elaborately chased, were scattered about. Richly embroidered hangings were suspended at several points, and a great fan, made from the feathers of some gorgeously plumaged bird, lay upon a sort of stand. He even thought he could distinguish several female garments thrown carelessly upon the couch. Way to descend among all this magnificence there was none. No interior stairway of any kind was visible, and it was quite evident that he who should be hardy enough to spring down would be caught like a rat in a trap.

Well, he had seen all he could see, and it was entirely incomprehensible. Now it was time to consult prudence and make up for his indiscretion by running no further risks. He rose and stood erect upon the roof. The dull boom of a distant cannon rolled up from the harbour, and then the sound of a musket discharged at regular intervals. Doubtless his companions were becoming alarmed at his stay. Perhaps they had learned that he had not reached the city, and, assuming him to be lost, were signalling to guide his return. In any case, it was beyond all question that a search would be promptly inaugurated. Hurrying down the winding stair, Vance ran across the clearing in the direction of the mountain, but just before plunging again into the woods he observed that he crossed what seemed to be an artificial boundary line composed of two parallel rows of black and white stones laid close together, the black forming the row nearer the ascent, the white the row nearer the open country adjoining the city. Then he

found himself once more surrounded by the
dense shadows of the woods, where the blood
ceased to bound in his pulses at every discharge of the signal guns that boomed now and
again from the shore.

Gradually, as he pressed on, the ascent became steeper; the trees were sparser and more
dwarfed; bare ledges of lava-like rock began
to appear, from several of which he could see
over the forest to where the *Falcon* still swung
at anchor. From one point he even made out
two boats rowing toward the shore. Captain
French evidently would not get away that
day, and Vance smiled as he pictured the wrath
of his commander.

At that moment a faint groan came to his
ears.

7

CHAPTER IX

LIRRHI

THE fugitive started at the sound, and listened intently. In a few moments he heard it repeated, and then an unmistakable though faint cry for help, as if muffled by distance, weakness, or some intervening obstacles.

For an instant he hesitated. Hitherto he had had no opportunity to think much, and his plans had looked only to escaping from the ship, without any definite idea as to how his solitary presence could avail to ward off from the Princess the vague dangers which he imagined encompassed her. Now it was necessary above all that no false step should be taken, and he fully realised that the disclosure to anyone of his presence on the mountain might be fraught with serious consequences.

Again the cry was repeated, more feebly

than before, and Vance found that he had not
the heart to be politic in such an emergency.
Someone was evidently in serious trouble; be
the results what they might, he must afford
what aid he could.

Fixed in this resolve, but not venturing to
return the call, he began to pick his way
cautiously in the direction whence the cries
had come. After a few steps he halted in
order to get new bearings,—fortunately enough,
as the event proved, for at that moment another
groan seemed to rise from directly beneath his
feet.

He felt the blood leap to his heart. Then
he composed his startled nerves and, parting
the bushes, prepared to move forward again.

His first step solved the mystery. He found
himself looking down into a narrow, deep
gully, apparently the bed of some dry stream,
and he realised how little less than providential
it was that he had not been pushing rapidly
forward as before, in which event nothing could
have saved him from falling into the snare and
being plunged down the steep declivity to
some such fate as he at once assumed must

have befallen the unfortunate whose voice had
guided him thither.

Peering over the edge, Vance at last made
out the figure of a man seated with his back
against a large boulder. At the same moment
the other, roused by the rustle of the leaves
above, looked up, revealing, as he did so, the
shaven head and dark face of one of the island
priesthood. The red tunic and black cloak
were there also, but the flame-tipped fillet was
gone,—probably dashed from his brow by the
fall.

An exclamation of joy from the Karanian
dispelled at once the feeling of aversion which
had for the moment prompted the American
almost to regret his humanity. Pushing the
bushes aside, he clambered carefully down the
decline and stood over the half-prostrate figure.

" What is the matter, my friend ? " he asked.

" I am Lirrhi the priest. I fell. I did not
see the ravine," was the reply; " and I am
hurt here and here." He indicated his left
arm and side.

Vance knelt down at once and began to strip
off the torn tunic. A hasty examination made

it evident that an arm and at least one rib were broken.

During this examination the priest eyed him with a curiosity which seemed more potent than the pain of his injuries, but he asked no question. Vance, too, had now an opportunity to observe the patient closely. He found him to be not more than thirty-five years of age, tall and powerfully built, and with a face in which the unpleasant characteristics he had noted as prevailing among his caste were entirely lacking. The man would have been called handsome anywhere, with his broad forehead, straight nose, and black, piercing eyes.

" Well," said the Lieutenant, as he finished his examination, " the first thing to do is to get you out of this hole. I suppose you can't help yourself very much ? "

" I have tried to climb out. Once I fainted from pain," was the reply.

Vance proceeded to busy himself about his task. He tore the priest's robe into strips and constructed a sort of sling, which he passed under the armpits of the injured man in such a way as not to strain or bind upon his hurts.

Then, running the other end of the improvised rope around a sapling growing upon the edge of the gully, he grasped it tightly in one hand, and, lifting the Karanian in his arms, began the hazardous ascent. Once or twice he slipped and the man groaned faintly, but Vance held fast to the strip of rope, and, balancing his own weight upon the other end, saved both from rolling back down the decline, until at last, half climbing and half drawing his burden up, he reached the top. The priest had fainted again from pain and exertion, but a few drops from the Lieutenant's flask seemed to revive him, and the latter at once set himself to bind up his patient's hurts as well as was practicable, tearing his shirt for the bandages and cutting rough splints from the neighbouring bushes.

After three-quarters of an hour's hard work the amateur surgeon surveyed the result with considerable self-satisfaction. The broken rib appeared to be well in place and so supported as to be likely to remain so; while the arm, only one of the small bones of which happened to be fractured, was set and splinted in so

masterly a way that he found himself wish-
ing that Deshon were there to admire his
handicraft.

By this time night was rapidly approaching,
and Vance began to vex himself with the
serious problem of how to dispose of his charge
satisfactorily without imperilling his own safety
or the success of the plans he must soon form.
The man had as yet said very little. His mind
seemed to be absorbed in some line of thought
from which terror was not altogether absent.
Still, Vance reasoned that gratitude must mean
something even with these fellows, and he determined to tell enough of his predicament to
find out whether the other could suggest any
mutually safe expedient.

Acting upon this resolve, he related in a few
words how he had deserted from his ship and
how he was undoubtedly being sought for and
must on no account allow himself to be taken.
Of his motives he thought it best to say
nothing.

The priest listened without interruption,
and, when Vance had finished, he said:

" I now understand why you dared venture

upon the sacred land of Tao. It is certain that none of our people will pursue you here, nor will they allow your countrymen to commit such a sacrilege."

Vance stared at the speaker in astonishment not unmingled with a satisfaction at the apparent assurance of at least temporary safety which the words conveyed, but Lirrhi proceeded to follow them up with an earnest appeal that the stranger would complete his good offices by assisting him to reach the foot of the mountain.

" There is a house," he continued, " not far from the boundary of black and white stones, where we can spend the night and find food. My brothers use it when they come to speak with Tao."

" But you are asking me," exclaimed Vance, " to leave the mountain, where you have just admitted that no one can follow me. Here at least I am safe. In the house you speak of I might be captured at any moment."

The face of the priest grew ashy, and there was a gleam of terror in his eyes. He seized Vance's hand.

"You must aid me to get away," he said. "If I should die here! If I should be found here thus! Do not fear to go. Fear rather to stay. I cannot tell you why, but trust yourself to me, who owe you more than my life." In an agony of agitation, he struggled to his feet, as if to make the attempt alone in case his rescuer should refuse to aid his descent.

"Well," thought Vance, "I suppose the place that 's safe for me is just the one that is n't safe for you, and *vice versa.*" A few moments of reflection, however, convinced him that it was wise as well as humane to comply with the other's wishes, and, if possible, bind him closer to his interests, even at the price of taking some risks. Such an ally might prove invaluable, and, in any event, it would never do to lose track of the man before satisfying himself on some points upon which his future plans must depend.

"Come, then," he said, passing his arm around Lirrhi so as to support his weight. "I will trust you. Tell me how to go."

For answer the priest carried the hand, which he still held, to his forehead, in token apparently of gratitude, and then, assisted by the fugitive, commenced the descent.

Their progress was necessarily slow, for the greatest care was required to avoid displacing the bandages or the set bones. Then, too, the forest was very dark, and nothing but the rays of the full moon made it possible for them to overcome in safety the many obstacles that beset their path. At last the ground became level, the lines of a low building loomed up before them, and the next moment Vance perceived that they were crossing the same boundary line of black and white stones which he had observed near the circular temple. It flashed across him that this must be designed to separate from the surrounding country the sacred ground to which the priest had alluded, and he greeted the surmise with a satisfaction which saw in it a piece of possibly very valuable knowledge to be utilised in such future emergencies as might arise.

They now entered the house, which proved to be a low structure of black stone, fitted up with considerable regard for comfort and well provisioned with dried fruits and such other

edibles as readily admitted of preservation.
From the moment of crossing the boundary a
marked change had come over Lirrhi's demeanour. He seemed like a man relieved
suddenly from some absorbing terror that had
hampered both his speech and his thoughts.
Slipping from Vance's arm and throwing himself at his benefactor's feet, he seized the
American's hand. His former preoccupied
silence was broken, and he now poured forth
expressions of gratitude so profuse that they
began to seem to their recipient entirely out
of proportion to even the service he had
rendered.

" Do you, who have saved more than my
life," he cried, " take its ordering to yourself.
I am your slave, with all that you have saved
to me." And again he pressed Vance's hand
to his forehead.

.The latter concluded to utilise so favourable
a moment for the obtaining of information.
" Doubtless you would have been found by
someone else," he suggested, " had I not
happened to pass."

The priest shook his head. " I had been

there for one night," he replied. " No one but a priest dare venture upon the mountain, and he whom Tao had snared could look for no aid from such. Had I died!— " He put his hand to his face and shuddered.

" I suppose it would have been rather unpleasant," said Vance.

" Do you not know," pursued the other, quickly, grasping the Lieutenant's wrist, "that, had my breathless body polluted the holy precincts but for a single moment, Tao would have consumed both it and my spirit in his fires ? Our laws even order him who may be hurt there, and yet escape, to be slain outright and thrown to the god, that he be not cheated of a feast he has prepared for. Should Aroo guess the truth, then, I were still lost; for he hates and fears me because my father, whom he slew, was once his rival for the office of high-priest."

Vance looked curiously at the man. Evidently he was not acting. His emotion was too real.

" You tell me," he said, " that all I have saved is mine, and you say I have saved your spirit from torture. Should I ask you to go upon the mountain and kill yourself—what then ? ''

The priest trembled, but he answered, firmly :

'' I would go. Both my life and my spirit's life were lost. You have found them and lent them to me. How should I refuse to repay the loan ? ''

Vance said nothing, but helped his patient to one of the couches, propped him up in as comfortable a position as possible, and began to investigate the larder. Hitherto action and anxiety had kept him from realising his wants, but now hunger asserted itself very forcibly. His companion, too, he felt must be in need of food after a fast of twenty-four hours. Fruits and a stone vessel containing some of the thick, sweet wine he had tasted at the banquet were soon procured, and they proceeded to eat and drink, Lirrhi sparingly, Vance with all the hunger of a healthy man who had been draw-ing on his nerves all day.

While thus employed, the American's mind was busy with several ideas. What could he lose by making a confidant of this islander whom he had befriended and whom Aroo had injured so deeply ?   Surely nothing ; and, while of course the possible gain could only be conjectured, he would at least be likely to learn something definite about the mysterious influences that opposed him.   Quickly taking his resolution, he turned to the priest, and, without any circumlocution or concealment, related to him, in as few words as possible, all that had happened, with the sole exception of his interview with the Soveet's daughter.   He told of his feelings upon seeing her at the banquet, his determination to win her, his interview with the Soveet and the high-priest, his deep impression that something lay behind their refusal which seriously menaced the girl herself, and his final determination to remain and either save her or share her fate.

His hearer listened attentively to this narrative of hopes, fears, and vague determination. When Vance had finished, he remained silent for several minutes.   The American's brow clouded with impatience.

" What would you that I should say ? "

asked Lirrhi mildly, as he noted the other's mood.

" The truth," cried Vance.

" Then, my friend, I beg of you to put this wish forever from your thoughts. It is hopeless,—as hopeless as that you should compel the mountain of Tao to discharge its molten fire under the sea."

But Vance was now in no humour to be satisfied with vague figures of speech. He went on in a tone which left no doubt of his set resolve to know all, and at once.

" You say that you are indebted to me—that you are my friend and Aroo's enemy. If you speak truly, then tell me exactly why I must put hope aside. If the reason appears to me good, I may follow your advice."

Lirrhi seemed deeply agitated. At last he fixed his eyes sadly upon his benefactor and replied, " The Princess Zelkah is consecrated to a higher fate than mortal nuptials."

Vance felt his blood chill, more at the manner than at the words.

" Go on. Explain; tell me all," he cried. " I have heard that much before."

" It is a long story—if you are to understand it," said the priest hesitatingly.

" Tell it, if it be from the beginning of the
world," was the reply; and Lirrhi, the priest
of Tao, began his tale, as follows:

CHAPTER X

TAO

" MANY years ago, the god Tao was pos- sessed of all the earth, and pervaded it in every part, so that in time he became the earth itself, devouring again and again the increase of flesh and corn and fruit and herbs and wood, that sprang from his own bosom fresh from each devouring.

" At last, however, Tao determined that he would no longer consume all things that grew, but that he would create man to be his friend and servant and worshipper, and endow him with the fruits of the earth, whereby he should live out his days.

" In order that this might be, the god sought out a special spot where he might dwell, in- stead of pervading all things; wherefore he selected the great mountain upon the island of

8

Karana which was then known by another name,—a name that no man may now speak and live. This spot he chose because the people whom he had created and placed here proved to be the most faithful and devout of all the many peoples he had created, and he knew that among them he need dread no interference with the land which he had reserved to himself when he gave all the rest to man.

" So Tao was an earth-god, and the animals wandered, and the trees grew upon his bosom, and died and were devoured by him and grew thence again, and the people dwelt upon the plains, and worshipped him, and slew animals upon his breast that their blood might sink down and nourish him the more bounteously; and Tao, in return for these things, watched over the people day and night and protected them.

" At last there came a day of new fortunes. One morning, when our fathers went down to the ocean, they saw a great canoe advancing toward the shore, with a great square sail and a horse's head at the prow and three tiers of

long oars that churned all the sea into white
foam. And men and women and children
with fair faces issued from the ship and descended upon the beach; and the men wore
bright metal upon their heads and bodies, and
their beards were black and bushy, and their
noses were curved like the beaks of eagles.

"Then did my people greet the strangers
kindly and give them land whereupon to live
and build houses; and the men from the sea
built the city and called it Karana; and they
were learned in many arts of which the islanders knew nothing, and introduced much wealth
and many strange customs, and taught the
people of the land, who learned gladly of them
and gave them due reverence and, later, power;
until, at last, the strangers came to rule over
the island, and chose, at first two of their number, whom they called soveets, and who, with
the help of a council of elders, governed both
races and made laws.

"At first, as you may imagine, they were
kindly and beneficent, and dealt fairly with us,
but when their numbers and power increased
we fell more and more under subjection, and

they became lords of the island and we their servants—little better than their slaves.

" And yet, through all, they did not interfere with the worship of Tao, but rather yielded obedience to him. Had they done differently, they would have been thrown back into the sea, despite their brass armour and sharp swords; for the people of the old race outnumbered the new a thousandfold, and still outnumber them many times, even after all these generations; and they would abide no failure of the worship of him who had fed and watched over them from the beginning of the years. So the strangers, seeing this, and being determined to rule, gave up one by one their own gods whom they had left behind them over the sea and worshipped Tao with us, and established a priesthood of our own race, that we might seek advancement so and not trouble ourselves about the government.

" It was not long, however, before many disputes arose between the priests of Tao and the descendants of the strangers, the priests setting up their word in many matters which the others would not permit, and all the people

were divided; for the strangers also worshipped
our god, and many of us were beholden to
them for much, so that, strive as they might,
the priests could not attain the power they
wished nor compel all the people of their blood
to support them to all lengths against the
soveets. Thereupon they did not love the
soveets, but were anxious to humiliate them
whenever the opportunity should be given.

" And now, while affairs stood thus, a strange
thing happened. The mountain, where dwelt
the god Tao, began suddenly to belch forth
fire and smoke and streams of molten rock that
flowed over the level ground and destroyed
crops and houses and killed men and animals
far and near, until a great terror came on the
land. One of the soveets who then ruled was
a proud man, and the high-priest had opposed
him in vain, and lost even much of the power
that his predecessors had, for the Soveet was
cunning and won our own people away from
his rival; and the high-priest hated the Soveet.
So, when the throat of Tao began to spread
destruction through the island, the high-priest
proclaimed everywhere that the god was angry

because of injuries done to the power and dignity of his children, the priests, in that they were subject to strangers; and all of his race, being very much in fear lest the island might be consumed away, believed what the high-priest said, for he was known to be a man of great piety and learning and well taught even in all the arts of the men from the sea.

" So at last all of the old blood gathered together and beset the soveets, and threatened to kill them and all their people unless they so dealt with the priests as to take away the wrath of Tao; and they besieged the soveets in their city until they and their followers had no food to eat. Then these came to terms and ratified the terms with oaths, and they and their council placed their children in the hands of the priests as hostages that they would make such reparation even as Tao might demand; only the head Soveet warned the high-priest, in the hearing of all the people, that if he and his did what the other commanded, then the curse of fire must be lifted, or the high-priest should stand forth and suffer punishment as an impostor who presumed to speak the words

of a god who spoke not to him. This condition also the people compelled the priests to
accept and to ratify with oaths.

" Thereupon the high-priest took fifty of his
followers and withdrew with them up into the
mountain, leaving orders that no man should
presume to follow; as, in fact, none were likely
to do, with the streams of burning mud pour-
ing down through the channels they had fur-
rowed out and threatening to spread over and
consume all. For a hundred days did the
high-priest and those with him remain hidden,
being seen by no man for the taboo which was
set upon the mountain.

"After they had been there one hundred
days, suddenly the flames ceased to come forth
for a whole day, and the people began to give
thanks; but soon they saw that they were not
yet safe, for Tao seemed to grow more angry
than ever, and then the priests descended the
mountain and came to the city and sought the
soveets, and the high-priest spoke, saying that
Tao had commanded, first, that the priests
should be held equal in power and honour to
the well-born, as the men from the sea were

called; and, second, that there should be but one soveet, who should rule with the high-priest, and, third, that it was Tao's pleasure that this soveet should give the most beautiful of his daughters to be the god's wife.

" As you may imagine, the head Soveet, being he who should remain in power, exclaimed loudly against such a penance, but the high-priest smiled and said it was no penance, but that the maid, in so dying, would bring high honour to herself and her father and his people.

" Again the Soveet cried out that this was the work, not of the god, but of the high-priest, who hated him and sought thus to be avenged; but the other smiled once more, and reminded him that if the Soveet spoke truth and no good came of the sacrifice the high-priest's head must answer for his deception. At these words, all of the old race, together with many of the Soveet's blood who saw no peril to themselves in this atonement, cried out that the high-priest spoke fairly, and that the life of a single virgin was a small matter compared with the safety of all the people.

" So the Soveet was compelled to yield, and

he gave his daughter over to the high-priest,
who had already built the circular house which
lies at the foot of the mountain to be a nuptial
chamber of the god; and they lowered the
maiden through the orifice in the roof, and,
with her, provisions for three days, and left
her there that the god might view her and take
her to his bosom in such season as he willed;
and they set a guard of thirty priests around
the house.

"The three days passed, and the maiden
cried out with hunger, and the Soveet, her
father, who was in great trouble, besought the
high-priest that she might be slain outright
and thus offered up to the god; but the high-
priest smiled and replied that no blemish of a
violent death must be upon the body of the
virgin bride of Tao. So the Soveet could gain
nothing, and the cries of the girl grew fainter,
until they could be heard no more.

"Then everything happened as the high-
priest had foretold; for Tao, being thus
appeased, ceased suddenly to devastate the
country with his burning breath, and withdrew beneath the mountain to find solace with

the spirit of the bride that had been offered to him.

" And the people gave thanks to the god, and, under him, to the Soveet, who had given his daughter to save them ; but above all they honoured the wise high-priest who had learned the will of Tao.

" For a time it was noticed that that part of the ocean that lay beyond the mountain boiled and was much troubled, but at last it too became quiet, and all the fears passed away.

" So it happened that there remained but one soveet, who ruled together with the high-priest, and this has been so ever since. The priests are in all respects equal to the well-born ; but the high-priest, by the help of 'Tao, is greater than the soveet; for whenever it has happened that the latter has been slow to govern as the former willed, then the god grows angry and belches up flame and smoke and molten rocks, until the soveet's daughter, clad in her richest robes, is taken in solemn pageant to the house by the mountain and left there to become the wife of Tao."

Vance had listened to this strange story of

superstition and barbarity with feelings he could hardly describe. His anger, his abhorrence, were too deep for words, and he was astonished at his own calmness.

" Do you mean, then, to tell me," he said slowly, as Lirrhi finished speaking, " that Zelkah, the daughter of your present Soveet, is reserved for such a fate as this ? "

" She is his only daughter," replied the priest; " and were she wedded and taken away there would be no one to appease Tao should his wrath break forth. No; even should Aroo, the high-priest, consent, the people would not permit it, nor the Soveet dare as much. He could not count upon the support of his own blood in such a quarrel."

" Well," said Vance, with that almost flippant composure which seems to come over an American when he feels most deeply, " all I 've got to say is that there will be a decided hitch in the arrangements if your priests attempt any such business while I 'm alive and here."

Unconsciously he had spoken in English, but Lirrhi seemed to catch the drift of the thought, and shook his head.

" You will fail," he said, " and you will die. You may even hasten her death, should Aroo suspect your designs."

" He does," said Vance, shortly.

The priest made no reply; and a few moments later he seemed to have fallen asleep, exhausted by pain, privations, and fatigue.

CHAPTER XI

NHAR

VANCE threw himself down upon a couch and endeavoured to sleep, but the horror of all that he now knew seemed to grow momentarily more present to him. Gradually he began to realise what it meant, and to measure his own helplessness. What could he accomplish but his own death in addition to that of the Princess? Under the spell of such thoughts, it would have been strange had even exhaustion closed his eyelids.

So the night dragged along. At last the blackness commenced to shade into grey. He could make out the form of his companion extended upon the other couch. The priest's face was turned toward him, and, as the light increased, Vance became conscious that the black eyes had been open for some time and were regarding him closely.

A fancy flashed across his mind that this might be the set glare of death; but, no, there was a look of deep concern on the face, and with it an expression such as a man wears when conflicting thoughts are warring in his brain. As for himself, he felt that his own appearance must be sufficiently haggard and drawn to excite the sympathy of even his enemies.

Lirrhi at last broke the silence.

" Tell me," he said, " are you still resolved to destroy yourself, now that you have slept and are rested ? Perhaps the gods that speak in sleep have taught you wisdom."

"I have not slept," said Vance very quietly; " but my purpose is not likely to change."

The manner and tone seemed to carry a conviction stronger than any violent words. The priest felt it. His brow contracted still more and he turned his face toward the wall. Then in a few moments he again bent his eyes upon the Lieutenant and there was a look of set resolve in them.

" Listen," he said. " You have determined. I, too, have thought and determined. I will help you, in return for what you have done for me, and for hatred of my father's slayer."

Vance sprang up and grasped the hand of the speaker. Then his face clouded again.

" What can you do more than I, my poor friend ? You will only involve yourself in my destruction," he said hopelessly.

Lirrhi's eyes flashed.

" What then ? " he replied. " Have not you saved me from death and worse ? Is not my life still in your hands ? It may happen that, with my aid, there will be new chances to favour you of which you cannot dream. There is danger for both of us and we may fail, but there may also be hope. No, do not question me," he continued, as the American's face gleamed with eagerness. " I make that a condition,—that you shall do my bidding and ask no questions. Shall it be so ? "

Such a proposition was not one to be weighed for a moment by a desperate man. Having no plan himself nor the prospect of any, surely he surrendered nothing in agreeing to adopt the plan of a person who had one. Besides, if it failed, he could still cut loose and make his own fight. Therefore Vance did not waste time in reflection.

" I accept," he said; " and I will obey you without question, so long as there is a chance of success. I only reserve the right to fight in my own way if—if— " he hesitated and then went on rather desperately —" should the Princess be threatened with any immediate danger."

" Very well," resumed the priest, ignoring the other's reservation. " I perceive that you are a wise man. Now attend. There is one who will be here soon and who will guide you to a place of safety where you must remain until I send for you. Hark! Surely that is his step now."

Vance listened anxiously, and soon even his duller ears caught the sound of a soft footfall. In a moment the door was pushed gently open and a pair of bright, bead-like eyes peered in. Their owner was a boy of apparently about fourteen years, with a slender, graceful figure, and dark-skinned like the native race. He started back in alarm when he descried the American.

" Do not fear, Nhar," said Lirrhi, raising himself upon the couch.

At these words the boy came forward again, glancing with an expression of solicitous inquiry toward where the priest lay. He made an obeisance but said nothing.

" I have been hurt, Nhar," continued Lirrhi, " and this man has saved me—perhaps from death. I wish, therefore, that he be taken to a place of safety from those that search for him, and concealed and cared for, and that you speak of his presence to no one — not even to Aroo himself. You know the cave upon the breast of Tao ? "

The boy nodded, shuddering slightly.

" That will be safe. Are the stranger's people doing aught ? Tell me what has happened."

Thus questioned, Nhar broke silence for the first time, speaking eagerly and with eyes full of wonder:

" Yes; their leader went to the Soveet and seemed by signs to accuse him of making away with the man, and there were violent gestures, and the leader of the strangers has sent forth

9

many armed bands into the woods to search, but the Soveet forbade that they be suffered to set foot upon the mountain, though they should threaten to destroy the town and kill everyone; but nothing has come of it yet, and the high-priest has ordered his followers to surround Tao and permit no one to enter there—— "

" Then you must be quick," interrupted Lirrhi. " Take him to the cave. See that he is supplied with food and drink, cover the entrance with boughs, and come back to me."

Vance was not loath, in view of the news he had heard, to return to the precincts which he had come to regard as a city of refuge; and, bidding Lirrhi a hasty farewell, with a parting word to the effect that he relied upon his promise of aid, the fugitive resigned himself to the pilotage of his young guide.

They started out at once, the boy leading the way along a new path, but resisting every effort of the American to draw him into conversation or to learn more about the condition of affairs at the city and the shore. He

seemed to have construed Lirrhi's command
of silence in its broadest sense. Soon they
crossed the boundary of black and white stones
and commenced the ascent, circling the mountain gradually toward the south, as if to place
its peak between them and the landing.

Finally, when they had reached a point
about two-thirds of the way up the western
slope, from which the city was not visible,
Nhar stopped suddenly and began to go carefully over the ground, like a hound looking for
a lost scent. Then he climbed a few steps
higher and, bending down, put aside the
boughs of a small tree, disclosing as he did
so a narrow opening. Motioning Vance to
hold the branches back, he stepped within
and, taking a lamp from a niche in the
rock, lighted it. They found themselves in a
medium-sized chamber hewn out of the stone
and provided with a couch and such simple
furniture and fittings as would suffice to make
an inmate reasonably comfortable. Dried
fruit, bread, and smoked meat stocked a larder
at least as luxurious as that of the house where
they had left Lirrhi.

Then, for the first time since they had started, Nhar spoke.

" Stay here," he said, " until I come. No one will find you. There is food enough for several days, and Lirrhi will take care of you."

Before Vance could reply with thanks, much less attempt to take advantage of this sudden communicativeness, the boy had left him and was bounding away down the mountain. When he had disappeared, the fugitive re-entered his place of refuge and proceeded to make himself as fully at home as circumstances would permit.

The two days that followed were dreary enough. There was absolutely nothing he could do, nothing to read, nothing even to think of, for his affairs had been taken so entirely out of his own hands that he felt himself a mere puppet to be moved when some controlling power pulled the strings. And yet, whenever his mind revolted against these conditions, it was only to find himself confronted with the alternative of attempting to carry Zelkah away by his own unaided force, against at least several thousand swords—and to carry her—whither ? It was preposterous. Simple suicide would be much more sensible. This was the conclusion upon which he was driven a hundred times as the days passed.

At last, when the mental agony of his position was becoming absolutely unbearable, and the third day was almost gone, Vance started from the couch on which he was reclining to see Nhar brush aside the concealing foliage and step down into the cave. Experience had, however, taught the American that it was useless to try to force this strangely reticent boy with questions, so he simply waited for him to speak of his own accord.

" Your people have gone away," said Nhar at last, after he had carefully inspected everything in the apartment, including its occupant.

At first Vance hardly knew whether to be glad or sorry. The news, of course, freed him from his most immediate peril and removed the first obstacle from his path; and yet the sensation of absolute loneliness that came over him—the consciousness that he was now but a single stranger amid a hostile race—drove the feeling of satisfaction from his mind.

Nhar watched his face curiously for a while. Then he continued:

"Lirrhi is waiting for you below.   Let us go down to him."

Mechanically Vance rose to his feet and, following the boy out of the cave, commenced the descent of the mountain.   As he turned the cliff fronting the harbour, he imagined he saw far down upon the horizon the glint of a white sail in the sunset.   Yes, he was now truly alone.

As they drew near to the house where he had left the priest, they saw a covered litter resting at the entrance and four sturdy fellows lounging against the wall.   A hand from within thrust aside the curtains and beckoned Vance to approach.   The black eyes of Lirrhi peered out at him and the priest's finger was at his lips.   The Lieutenant bent down.

"You are better?" he said.   "Your hurts are healing?"

"Yes; much better—nearly well, I think," replied the other, hurriedly; "but a word with you before the bearers come near.   Say nothing of your or my whereabouts for these

days; above all, say nothing of the mountain
or of how I received my injury. Leave everything to me. You strayed away and were lost
—do you understand ? It is necessary. The
Soveet was rudely used by your people and he
must never know that you remained willingly.
He may suspect. He may think you a fool.
So much the better. But should Aroo dream
the truth, we are both dead men. Say as
little as you can.''

The American nodded, to indicate that he
understood the warnings. The bearers came
forward, and, raising the litter upon their
shoulders, commenced the journey to the city.
Vance and Nhar walked one on each side, or,
where the path became too narrow, behind,
but no further words were spoken and no
sound broke the stillness save the dull monotonous croon to which the litter-men timed
their steps.

It was dark when they entered the gate, a
circumstance which it flashed across Vance's
mind had probably been planned for by Lirrhi
and which tended to inspire a confidence in
the prudence of his ally.

It soon appeared, however, that all measures to conceal his presence had been vain, for scarcely had they reached a small house in one of the side streets and, carrying the priest within, laid him on a bed, when a thundering of staves sounded upon the door.

Vance started to his feet and began to examine his revolvers, but Lirrhi signed to him that he should do nothing rash, and ordered Nhar to attend the summons.

A dozen men carrying torches and a litter were disclosed without, and Vance's astonishment was unbounded to see the Soveet himself part the curtains of the latter and step down.

After giving some command to his attendants, the prince advanced to the door, entered hastily and closed it behind him. Then he looked thoughtfully from one to the other of the inmates, — Lirrhi upon the couch, and Vance and Nhar seated near its foot. At last he spoke.

" I found it difficult to believe the word brought me,—that you had returned here," he said slowly. " Therefore I came myself to make sure."

No one answered. After a pause, he continued:

" Your course has resulted in grave trouble to me and my people. I have been accused of killing you or of imprisoning you,— I know not which; but your master was pleased to make all the threats that signs could carry, threats of what he would do unless I produced you. His men and mine searched earnestly, except upon the sacred mountain, and there was well-nigh war when we would not suffer that he should search there also."

The Soveet cast an inquiring glance at the American, as if expecting some reply, but Lirrhi hastened to forestall his words.

" The stranger is under the protection of Tao himself," he said. " He was honoured by the god in being selected to save me, his priest, perhaps from death."

The Soveet started in surprise, and Lirrhi continued:

" You may well believe, then, that Tao would protect him from all pursuers and wheresoever he might best do so. That protection must be assured to him henceforth."

The Soveet played thoughtfully with a little gold dagger with a blade like a jet of flame that hung at his girdle.

" It is my wish," he said, at last, " to protect him as far as my power extends, despite the fact that he has so borne himself as to bring evil upon me and mine. That also is why I came here myself upon learning of his arrival. There is a house on the square near my own which I shall assign for his residence, and it is well that he should be established there to-night."

Vance glanced toward Lirrhi, but the latter merely bowed his acquiescence with impassive face.

" It is best, too, that you should come at once," resumed Merrak, and he turned as if to lead the way.

The priest leaned forward and spoke to Vance hurriedly and in a low tone:

" He is right. It is impossible for you to stay here without destroying my power to help you. I have been much troubled to know what to do, but the Soveet has solved the problem wisely. I am persuaded that he

wishes you well. Go with him quickly. You
are safe for the present, but do nothing till
you hear from me."

Their august visitor had reached the door;
now he glanced back impatiently. In a moment Vance was at his side and they stepped
out into the deserted street. It was evident
that the torch- and litter-bearers had been
ordered not to wait, and for a few minutes the
two men walked on in silence. The night was
very black, but Vance imagined that he saw
the shadows of dark faces and the gleam of
serpentine blades at every corner. Time and
again his hand sought, half unconsciously, the
butt of one of his pistols, till the touch restored his courage. He breathed a heartfelt
sigh of relief as they issued at last from gloomy
alleys and tombstone-like buildings into the
open square. Reaching the door of a small
house facing eastward, his guide opened it and
entered. A lamp burned upon a table, showing
an anteroom connected by a passage with what
appeared to be a bedroom beyond. The furniture was simple and the fittings plain, but
everything promised a considerable degree of

comfort. Having inspected the place carefully, Merrak turned to take his leave, and,
after a moment's hesitation, said :

" I wish you to understand that the protection which I now extend to you is upon
one condition. You must surrender at once
and forever your impossible hopes. You must
never even see my daughter. I do not know
what evil your actions may have already
brought upon her and my house, but I fear
much. That Aroo suspects and watches you
I am sure, and it would be strange did he not.
A suspicion is generally enough for one of his
kind, and I dread him most when he refrains
from striking."

For reply, Vance drew the Soveet back from
the door and then, looking him straight in the
eyes, said :

" Why will you not join with me in destroying this vermin of a priesthood ? It is cow-
ardly to fear and yield to them as you do."

Merrak seemed strangely agitated. He put
up his hands, as if to ward off the other's
words.

" No, no; you do not understand," he said,

speaking rapidly and in low tones. "They are all-powerful with the people,—even mine. I am nothing,—the god—— "

Vance could not suppress the look of contempt that crossed his face, but fortunately the dim light concealed it. He felt that to tell the weak man before him that he was fully acquainted with all the dangers he feared, would be only to betray his friend.

"As you please," he said shortly. "But *my* people are not accustomed to yield so readily. As for myself, I promise nothing."

"Then you will die, and she that you love with you. Aroo is cruel, and Lirrhi cannot save you, even if he would. Be warned."

Vance almost imagined for a moment that the old man was about to throw himself at his feet; but he rallied his dignity and stepped to the door, turning once again, before he disappeared in the darkness, to say, in tones so pleading as to be absolutely pitiful:

"It is one who would be your friend that says it. Be warned."

CHAPTER XII

FACE TO FACE

A S soon as the sound of the Soveet's footsteps had died away, Vance turned from
the door, first closing it and sliding home
the bolts with which it was well provided.
Then, taking up the lamp, he proceeded to
examine carefully his new residence—or prison
—with a view to estimating its defensive capa-
bilities in case of an attack.

His survey was entirely satisfactory. There
was nothing that could be set fire to. A few
narrow windows, or rather ventilators, opened
just beneath the roof, but it was quite evident
that they were much too small to admit the
body of a man or even to allow of successful
archery practice by enemies from without. The
door, then, was the only point to be guarded,
and he looked to his revolvers with a serene

confidence in their power to make good that position. Even if compelled to depend upon his sword, he reasoned that nothing but a con-certed rush on the part of men the foremost of whom were prepared to sacrifice themselves could prove of any avail; and still there would always be an opportunity to fall back into the inner room and defend the passage leading to it.

After all, however, there seemed to be but little reason to anticipate siege or assault, and, his examination completed and plan of defence formed, Vance placed his sword and pistols within easy reach and threw himself down upon the couch.

Weariness and vigorous health had begun to do their work, and he had almost yielded to the powers that induce slumber, when his senses, naturally acute, were aroused to their full activity by a sound that came to him from without — the quick tread of a sandalled foot upon the pavement.

In a moment he was up and listening in-tently, pistol in hand.

The steps came nearer, but the Lieutenant

was on the point of laughing at his sleepy imagination for transforming a belated wayfarer into a midnight assassin, when they stopped abruptly before his door. Then followed a moment of apparent hesitation on the part of the newcomer and of sharp tension on that of the waiting garrison.

Several times during his life Vance had noted that, however much he might bemoan his tendency to seem irresolute in trifling emergencies, yet whenever the call upon his courage and decision was definite and peremptory his nerves responded promptly and became firm as steel. In fact, he even imagined that he could think more clearly and appear and be cooler and more collected on such occasions than could most of the men whom he envied for their readiness of speech and action when nothing but ready speech or tactful action was required.

In the present situation and while he waited for the next development, it occurred to him that the danger of using his pistol in dealing with a single adversary would be much greater than that of taking his chances in a hand-to-

hand encounter. Therefore he slipped the
revolver into his belt again and cautiously
drew his sword.

Meanwhile, the stranger, whoever he might
be, had evidently decided upon his own course,
and, advancing boldly, struck two sharp blows
on the door.

" Who are you ? " asked Vance, with a
promptness which must have surprised his
visitor somewhat.

" Hush! do not speak so loudly," said the
other earnestly. "'Can you not open your
door to me ? "

Something in the man's voice struck the
American as familiar, and yet he found himself
unable to place it.

" I can open my door to you if I want to,"
replied he in lower tones; " but before I do
so you must pardon me if I ask again who
you are and what you desire."

" You are very cautious." There was a
sneering emphasis on the words which served
at once to refresh Vance's memory.

" Aha! my medical and priestly friend!
So it 's you, is it ? " he thought. " I don't
10

believe I am suffering from any special anxiety for a *tête-à-tête.*"

" I am Mapo and I bring you a message from the Lady Zelkah," went on the other hurriedly.

Vance felt himself trembling with eagerness where a moment before he had stood upon his guard, cool and collected. A few seconds of reflection, however, bade him be slow to admit the truth of his enemy's statement.

" Do not, I pray you, compel me to stand here," continued the alleged messenger. " I shall be seen by someone, and suspicion may rest upon me. I come to take you to the Princess."

Vance had by this time entirely recovered his self-control, and the last announcement merely made his blood course a little faster through his veins. He had already decided that there could be no especial risk in admitting one man, provided he kept him carefully under watch. Fixing a seat, therefore, and placing the lamp so that its rays would fall upon the face of his visitor, he slid back the bolts, opened the door, and stood to one side.

The priest entered, carrying a fair-sized

bundle under his arm, and took several steps into the room, glancing around to discover the whereabouts of his host. Vance seized the moment to close and bolt the door again. Then, as Mapo turned at the sound, he faced him and motioned to the seat. Had there been any treacherous design in the other's mind, he must have seen that the odds were all against its success, and, besides, he appeared to be unarmed.

" Your caution is needless," he said, seating himself with a supercilious smile. " Do you imagine that if we aimed at your life there would be any trouble about taking it ? "

" I think I might make a good deal of trouble for you before you got it," said Vance carelessly. " As for my caution, which you are pleased to sneer at, *I* prefer to be the judge of its necessity."

" And yet you will have to trust me if you wish to see her," said the other.

" That remains to be considered when I have learned who she is," replied Vance. " In the first place, pray deliver your message."

" My message is short," said the priest.

"It is the Lady Zelkah's wish to speak with you, and she bade me bring you to her presence."

"What proof have you that you are not devising a snare for me?" asked Vance. "It is a most remarkable summons, and why should your Princess desire an interview with a stranger whom she has hardly seen?"

"You seem to forget that your course has not been a secret," replied Mapo, again dropping into his sneering tones. "Aroo understands well this trick of your being lost,—a shallow one,—a very shallow one. You have been doing all you could to hasten the extinction of your own hopes, and I, the distrusted physician, alone offer you a chance to retrace your steps and perhaps even to set them in a wiser path."

"You are very benevolent," said Vance, bowing and realising that he had almost caught the supercilious manner of his visitor.

"No, I am not benevolent," said the priest, calmly. "I have objects of my own to attain, and perhaps we can help each other. Meanwhile I await your answer."

Vance had been thinking hard ever since
Mapo had announced his mission. He fully
realised that it was more than likely that its
object was to get the better of him in some
way and either capture or kill him or, worse
yet, to involve Zelkah herself by some devilish
piece of trickery. On the other hand, the
story might be true, and it was impossible to
foretell what chances might be thrown away
by not seizing such an opportunity. Against
personal violence his pistols and the mysterious
destruction they could spread seemed to offer
a fair defence. To be sure, it would be necessary, in a measure, to violate his agreement
with Lirrhi, but to that it could be said that
unforeseen circumstances had arisen, that his
ally might fully approve of his contemplated
action were there time to advise him of it, and
that, in short, he was very much in the position of an officer cut off from all communication with his commander-in-chief and called
upon, in a sudden emergency, to use his own
judgment, even to the extent of breaking
orders. The argument, however, which bore
most strongly on his decision was the desperate

nature of his enterprise and his consciousness that desperate chances must be taken at
every turn in order that no possible advantage
should be lost.

All this passed through the Lieutenant's
brain very rapidly and, looking the priest
straight in the face, he said:

" I have decided.   Lead on, and I will follow.   Only be sure that at the first suspicion
you are a dead man."

" You expose your benefactor to danger
from your own fears," sneered Mapo.   " However, I suppose I must take my chances.   I
had reserved this," he continued, commencing
to unroll his bundle, " in case you should need
further urging."

With these words he drew out and held
toward Vance a golden cincture not much over
three spans in circumference, which the latter
recognised at once as the belt Zelkah had worn
at the time of their short interview.   To be
sure, the priest's having it in his possession
did not necessarily mean that it had been given
him to be used as a pledge of good faith, but,
as Vance had come to his own determination

without knowing of its presence, he did not waste any time upon such considerations.

What the belt had been wrapped up in, he now saw, was a black cloak similar to those the priests wore, but considerably longer and provided with a hood.

"You must throw this about you," said Mapo, handing him the garment.

Vance complied, but without relaxing his grasp on his sword or allowing his eyes to stray from the movements of his companion. Then, unbolting and opening the door, he motioned to the priest to step out, following him closely as he did so and drawing the door to behind him. His guide halted for a moment and half turned.

"Lead on. I will follow you," said the American. There was a dangerous ring in his voice and he rested his sword on his hip at half-thrust with the point presented directly at the other's body.

Mapo gave vent to a half-sniff, half-grunt, which might have meant many things, and, turning quickly, led the way in the direction of the palace. No one was passing in the streets; the moonbeams played through the clouds upon the white pavement of the square and bathed the walls of the houses with floods of pale light.

To Vance's surprise, his guide hurried past the long, glittering front of the Soveet's dwelling and pushed on some distance beyond. Then, threading his way through several dark and narrow streets where every corner seemed a fit lurking-place for ambuscades, he returned by a half-circle, and, stopping before a small postern at the rear of the palace, rapped softly three times. The door was opened immediately by a heavily cloaked figure,—a very tolerable double of the American himself. The latter had taken the precaution to shift his sword to his left hand and to grasp one of his revolvers in his right so as to be armed to the best advantage in the event of a sudden attack in force. The sword might have sufficed for Mapo alone, but now perils were thickening at every step.

The priest had entered a low, dark passage, while the cloaked figure stood to one side, as if indicating that Vance also should pass.

There seemed to be no option.   He was in the
enemy's stronghold, and he felt that it would
be useless to attempt to keep all possible assailants in front.   Therefore, with scarce a
second's hesitation, he hurried after his guide
and heard the door through which he had entered close behind him.   Greatly to his relief,
its guardian did not follow them.

There was nothing to lighten the darkness
that shut him in, nothing to pilot him but the
walls of the narrow hallway and the sound of
his conductor's footsteps ahead.   He could
not help realising how easy it would be for the
latter to give him the slip at any moment, and
yet his nerves and courage grew firmer and
stronger as his power of defence against treachery became manifestly weaker.   Several times
the passage turned and finally it terminated at
a flight of stairs, of the presence of which Mapo
took care to give timely warning.   Then followed more passages and then more steps,
until suddenly they issued out into the open
air.

A glance about him showed the American
that they were on the roof of the palace, and

that a large portion of its surface was laid out in a sort of garden thick with waving, palm-like plants and glittering with the spray of fountains.

Vance turned inquiringly to his guide who had halted and faced him. The latter said nothing, but, raising his hand, pointed toward what seemed to be a structure of some kind that rose amid the thickest of the foliage. Then he threw himself down beside the opening in the roof through which they had ascended, and Vance, still holding his pistol cocked and ready for use, walked cautiously forward among the plants. In a moment he had reached a bower constructed of interlaced vines twined together so skilfully as to support each other without the aid of a sustaining lattice, and, as he paused at the entrance, another cloaked figure rose from a low seat and confronted him. Almost immediately the hood was thrown back, the mantle fell to her feet, and he stood face to face with Zelkah.

She was robed in a long black tunic, unbelted, with flowing sleeves, and entirely unrelieved by any embroidery or ornament. No costume could have been less graceful, but her head was bare and the single ray of moonlight that stole through the vines and fell upon her pale upturned face showed a beauty that the most disfiguring dress could not detract from.

Vance sprang forward with a short exclamation.   Then he stood stock-still before the look of scorn that flashed from her eyes. There was absolute silence for a few moments. At last she spoke:

"You have regarded my words well.   I thank you for permitting me to estimate the true value of your protestations."

Vance strove in vain to utter a word.   After a short pause she went on:

"Was it not the part of a man to hold sacred the wishes of one whom he professed to love ? But you have presumed on what was but a moment of weakness, induced by what magic I know not, to involve me in perils of which you cannot conceive."

"Is it to tell me this that you have sent for me ?" he said at last, regaining in a measure his power of speech, but still stunned and bewildered by her words.

" For this and to take back that which I told you to my shame. Were it even true that I could have loved you in such unmaidenly haste, without the aid of magic, be sure your mad actions would have dispelled all."

" What do you wish that I should do ? " said Vance, feeling and speaking as one in a dream.

Her face at once became animated with a strange eagerness and she made as if to step forward.

" Fly,—escape, and at once," she said.

" How ? " asked he quietly, while a new light began to dawn slowly upon his mind.

" Go to my father.   He will gladly give you a galley and crew, and you shall order them whithersoever you will," she continued in beseeching tones.

A lover's intuition had enabled Vance to understand what no reasoning could have availed for.   He made no reply, but sprang forward and caught her in his arms.   For a moment she struggled against him.   Then the tears burst from her eyes.

" How cruel you are! " she murmured.

" Cruel! " he said, speaking rapidly and in a voice vibrant with passion: " cruel to understand why you denied your own heart's words in order that I might be saved from peril,—to drive me away from you who are the only life I have or care to have! You could not play your part to the end, though. Your nature is too truthful for that."

She was very quiet now and made no effort to escape.

" What is death or suffering," he went on, eagerly, " beside the joy of a moment like this ? "

" It is nothing," she said, in the faintest of whispers, and then their lips met in a long kiss.

CHAPTER XIII

MAPO

IT was some moments before either could regain even a measure of the self-control that had been swept away so completely. Zelkah was the first to speak, and there was a note of deep dejection in her voice.

" Now, my beloved, it is indeed I who have bound you hand and foot and delivered you over to those who seek your death. Why could not my heart have been firm to hold by the wise words of Mapo, inspired though they were by evil ? "

A new train of ideas suddenly suggested itself to Vance.

" It was not you, then, lady, who devised this plan to send me away ? " he asked quickly.

There was a moment's hesitation. Then she said :

" No."

Just why the physician of the Soveet—a
member of the priestly caste—should interest
himself in the safety of a foreigner and an
enemy presented, for the moment, a puzzling
question to the American. Both his perceptions and his judgment, however, seemed
singularly clear on this night. It was certainly
not probable that the priests feared his power
and wished him away for their own sake. All
Aroo's actions distinctly negatived such a supposition, and the high-priest was, of course,
ignorant of the value of the weapons which
gave Vance the only advantage he possessed.
He was almost beginning to divine the solution
of the puzzle, in part at least, when Zelkah
spoke again.

"Listen," she said. "I will conceal nothing
from you. It was Mapo that came and spoke
of the perils to which your love exposed me
and tried to persuade me to send him to bring
you into my presence in order that I might
turn your love to hatred. Then, when I told
him that I feared no perils, and when I sought
to avoid his presence and words, he cunningly
suggested that you, too, would surely be

involved in my destruction, and explained that, if you could but be convinced that I despised you, your escape could be readily arranged. So I yielded; and you see how well I have carried out my purpose.''

Vance kissed her again.

'' But why does this man interest himself in my safety ? '' he asked, after a short silence.

She looked him full in the face and answered without hesitation :

'' It was not your safety that he desired ; it was mine.'' Then she went on, blushing faintly: '' I have often dreamed that he regarded me with a feeling the thought of which filled my whole soul with loathing. There were glances and stray words that told me this, and once he even had the presumption to say to me that a high-priest were no unfit mate for a soveet's daughter. I had heard that he aspired to succeed Aroo. Still, if I could save you, it mattered little whose help I invoked or how it was obtained.''

Vance smiled when she finished speaking. What did he care now for Aroo and Mapo and Merrak ? They were all as if leagues away.

" But, dearest," he said, " do you not see how little likely I would be to escape, even had you succeeded in your design and a galley been furnished ? Assuming that Merrak and Aroo had consented to such a proceeding, your sailors, accustomed only to these inland seas, would have had neither the will nor the courage to carry me the many days' journey necessary to gain a place of safety. It would be much easier to throw me into the sea and return with a tale of my arrival at my destination, and I have even grave doubts whether their orders, from Aroo at any rate, would not contain some such direction."

She looked at him, half terrified, while he was speaking, and when he had finished she said :

" But at least there would have been a chance. Here there is none."

" There would have been no chance then to hold you in my arms, as now," he laughed, " and that is worth far more than safety. Besides, the danger is not nearly what you dread. I have learned of all these horrors, and the very thought of them made my blood run

cold; but consider how many years are likely
to pass before your Tao may light his fires
again.   Until then, we have nothing to fear,
and when that time comes we shall doubtless
have died long before."

"But Tao breathes fire when he is angry,
and Mapo and Aroo have said that he is in-
dignant at what has already happened."

"Aroo and Mapo do not know all things,"
said Vance smiling.   "I imagine Mapo would
not be entirely pleased, could he see how little
his plots have availed him thus far."

He was debating with himself as to his ability to make clear to her the laws that governed
volcanic phenomena, when his ear caught a
rustle in the foliage behind him.

Zelkah heard it, too, and started from his
arms with an exclamation of terror, as Vance,
sword in hand, sprang quickly in the direction
whence the sound had issued.   Nothing was
to be seen or heard.   The branches and great
leaves of the palms were swaying slightly, but
whether disturbed by the passage of some
body or by the impulse of the breeze was
hard to tell.   After a short but thorough

search, he returned to where he had left
Zelkah.

The girl was trembling, and he tried in vain
to reassure her.

"You must go, and at once," she said,
earnestly. "It cannot be far from morning,
and even my father would kill you did he
know that I had so far offended as to seek this
interview. I will find means to communicate
further—unless—unless you will yet grant my
heart's prayer and fly from this terrible
land."

For answer Vance only laughed softly,
caught her once more in his arms, and kissed
her, until at last she succeeded in slipping
from him.

"Go now and go quickly, if you would obey
the least of my wishes," she said. "Above
all, be cautious in what you say to Mapo."

"I will go and I will be cautious," he answered; "but you must first tell me that you
will try to put away these vain fears. There
is a God who is able to bring to naught the
power of this Tao of yours."

"I will promise anything. I will be brave

and fear nothing and remember only that you love me.''

With this farewell, she turned and in a moment was lost amid the darkness and the shadows of the plants, while Vance, overcoming the lover's impulse to follow and seek yet one more word, began to pick his way cautiously toward where he had left his guide.

He found the priest reclining just as he had thrown himself down when they parted, and apparently buried in deep slumber,—so deep, in fact, that it was several seconds before Vance could arouse him. Then he started to his feet in a bewildered way. Altogether, the incident recalled to the Lieutenant's mind the sound that had startled Zelkah and himself. It seemed very unlikely that a man whose brain and heart were filled with the schemes and ambitions of which the Princess had spoken would fall calmly asleep at such a moment, and the manner of his awakening had about it a strong suggestion of overacting.

Concluding, however, that it would be unwise to show suspicion, Vance spoke jestingly of the other's somnolence, and suggested that it was time to make haste before daylight should overtake them.

" Perhaps you do not doubt my truth now," said Mapo, as he arose and settled his cloak. " Did the words of the Lady Zelkah bring you to better judgment ? "

Vance felt that, in the light of the knowledge obtained, he had a new part to play and one which demanded that he should appear to show a fuller confidence in his companion. He admitted that there was something of peril in this course, especially if his suspicions as to the man's eavesdropping were correct. Still, there was no choice. A certain amount of frankness about matters with which the other must be more or less familiar seemed also politic.

Therefore he drew his brows together and answered :

" Judgment is one thing, my friend, and the warm blood of youth is another. I have heard words to-night that filled me with sorrow and I must ponder before I decide what their influence shall be."

" Yes," said Mapo, reverting to his old

sneering tones; " the warm blood of youth is foolish, but it should at least know that it is better off when flowing within the body than when spattered over the stones."

They had now descended into the labyrinth of passages through which they had come, and Vance pressed closely after his guide. He breathed a sigh of relief to find himself at last passing through the narrow postern and out into the street. In accordance with his new policy, he now walked beside his companion, only falling back a step as they neared turns in the road, as if waiting to learn the proper direction. He had sheathed his sword, and his only precaution was to keep a sharp eye on the other and to hold his muscles in readiness to respond to any sudden call.

In this way they finally arrived at the house to which the Soveet had assigned him, and Vance, pushing open the door, entered quickly. He half turned to see if Mapo was going to take his leave, but it was evident that the priest had no such intention, for he followed the American in and, closing the door behind them, seated himself upon the same stool

which he had occupied before. Surmising
that the man had something further to say
and anxious to be rid of him as soon as possible, Vance also sat down and eyed him inquiringly. A short silence ensued, and then
Mapo spoke:

" Will the stranger follow the advice of the
Lady Zelkah ? "

" The stranger must have time to consider
somewhat," said Vance shortly; " but truly
there seems little for him to hope for here."

" There is *nothing* to hope for here," pursued
the other, bending forward and speaking in
lower tones, " except through me."

" What do you mean ? " queried Vance.

" This only: that, were Merrak dead, there
would be a new soveet, and Zelkah would be
free to marry whomsoever she would. If you
say the word, I can kill Merrak."

Vance was fairly startled out of his composure by this point-blank proposal. A moment
later, when he had gathered himself together
a little, he tried to divine the possible motive,
and found himself strongly inclined to doubt the
good faith of the Soveet's favourite physician,

or, more properly speaking, to doubt his *bad* faith to his master. To be sure, assuming that Mapo loved Zelkah, their interests would be identical up to the point of freeing the Princess from her terrible betrothal; and then, too, the crafty priest might have some scheme whereby Merrak's death could be charged to and ruin his rival. The longer he thought, the more he began to doubt his first conclusion, and to believe that the proposition, as far as it went, was entirely *bona fide*.

" Well, what word do you say—yes or no ? " asked Mapo sharply and apparently irritated by the thoughtful silence of the American.

" I say that you are even a more advanced scoundrel than I dreamed," said Vance, looking the other straight in the face. " What your motive is for such an offer I cannot imagine," he went on, craftily dissembling the results of his reflections; " but I am not accustomed to attacking even my enemies by such means. As for your Soveet, he has treated me most considerately, under circumstances—— "

Suddenly he became conscious that Mapo

was springing upon him. His early vigilance
had been somewhat relaxed, both from motives of policy and by something akin to confidence born of the absence of any suspicious
act on the priest's part. He knew that he
could have been readily stabbed in the dark
hallways of the palace, where the prick of the
steel would have been his first warning, yet he
had emerged safe and sound. Now his companion had chosen the moment when the
Lieutenant's mind was full of what he had just
heard and his attention absorbed in the words
he was uttering.

Before he could even get to his feet, the
priest was upon him, and in struggling to rise
Vance slipped and fell backward over the seat
upon which he had been sitting. It was
doubtless the accident alone that saved his
life, for by it he escaped the stab of a short
serpentine dagger which Mapo had plucked
from under his robe and with which he struck
viciously as he sprang.

The result of his fall, however, was even
more far-reaching than to preserve him from
the first thrust, for his assailant, expecting to

be met body to body and finding a vacuum where he had looked for resistance, stumbled and, striking the same stool with his foot, pitched forward upon the prostrate American, while the dagger slipped from his hand in his effort to preserve his equilibrium.

It was into a life-and-death struggle for the possession of this weapon that the fight now resolved itself. Mapo was uppermost, but Vance, whose presence of mind was, as I have said, always readiest in the greatest emergencies, caught the glitter of the steel where it lay and managed to give it a kick that sent it over into one corner of the room. Meanwhile he pressed the other close in his arms,—so close as not even to permit of the priest's getting a grip on the throat of the man beneath him or using his hands with any effect.

In this position they writhed and twisted about, the Karanian trying hard to free himself,—the American, to roll him over and get uppermost. Their strength was not very unequal, but it soon became evident that the white man was possessed of more endurance. The struggles of his enemy appeared to grow more feeble, and a moment later Vance twisted one leg around those of Mapo, and, exerting himself to his utmost, by a sudden effort turned the priest upon his back, at the same time breaking his hold and pushing himself away.

The advantage seemed to be his, but he had to do with a ready foe, for as the islander fell he caught sight of the hilt of Vance's sword, which the Lieutenant had been unable to draw, and grasping at it with both hands drew it from its scabbard just as its owner gained his feet and sprang back. Before Vance could begin a new struggle for this weapon, Mapo had bounded up and was advancing upon him with a smile of malicious triumph on his dark face.

To use his pistols the American still felt would be dangerous in many ways, and he boldly determined to continue the combat on the present lines at any cost. Surely he was no worse off than at first. With an agility for which he had not given himself credit, he darted across the room, stooped, and possessed himself of his enemy's dagger,—a poor weapon against a sword, but certainly much better than nothing.

Mapo crept forward cautiously and Vance, as he fell back and evaded him, soon saw that his adversary sought only to thrust, a purpose for which the islander's swords were best adapted.   He could guard this with his dagger better than he could a blow, and he was just meditating upon how to possess himself of the long cloak which he had worn that night and either wrap it about his arm or use it as the net of a retiarius, when his eye fell upon the stools on which they had been sitting.   At the same moment the priest leaped at him and thrust furiously, but Vance, parrying with his dagger, bounded to one side, and before the other could divine his intention he had picked up one of the stools and hurled it with all his force full at Mapo's head.   It was only a glancing blow, but, as the priest staggered and instinctively threw up both hands to ward it off, the American found his opportunity, and rushing forward plunged the dagger twice into his enemy's breast.

At least one of the thrusts must have struck

safely home, for the Karanian gave voice to a half-stifled, gurgling cry, and, sinking down upon the floor, twitched once or twice and then lay still. Vance stood looking at the body and panting from his long-continued and violent efforts. Then he wiped the dagger upon the long black mantle and, replacing it in the priest's bosom, proceeded to wrap the corpse up in the same garment. It must be disposed of somehow, he thought, and the now rapidly dawning light made it impossible to dream of carrying it away. There seemed to be nothing to do but roll it under the couch so that it might be hidden in case anyone should enter, to wash the splashes of blood from the floor, and to wait for the ensuing night to remove and bury it.

These things accomplished, bodily exhaustion proved all-powerful, and, throwing himself down upon the bed that concealed the body of his would-be murderer, Vance slept more soundly than he had since the day when the *Falcon* had first sighted the island of Karana.

CHAPTER XIV

THE BRIDAL SUMMONS

EXHAUSTED by fatigue and excitement, the American rested all day. Once he was aroused by a servant bringing food. Then he fell asleep again.

As the night closed in, his sleep became more troubled. Strange noises seemed to sound in his ears, and he dreamed that a great mob, composed of many thousands of dark-robed priests, was pursuing him, and that each was blowing upon a brazen trumpet, the notes of which seemed to shape themselves into his name. Just as they were about to overtake him, a crash of sound louder and nearer caused him to start from his slumber. In a moment he realised that some great commotion was taking place in the square without. The hum of many voices came to his ears, but low and indistinct, as if each were suppressed by some pervading sentiment of sorrow or terror. Suddenly a low, deep detonation rang out like the explosion of some distant magazine. Then a blare of trumpets, wild, fitful, and discordant, drowned all other sounds, to be followed again by the wailing of the crowd. As nearly as his aroused senses could locate it, the trumpet clangour came from the direction of the great black temple that stood near the Soveet's palace.

Vance sprang from his couch, and, approaching the window, looked out. He saw the torch-lit space before him packed through its whole length and breadth with a mass of humanity. Men and women of both races were mingled together, and upon such faces as he could distinguish was a look partly of awe, partly of deep dejection. Their eyes seemed bent upon some object above and beyond the building he occupied; and then a suspicion of the meaning of it all flashed through his mind.

Turning, he rushed to the rear part of his new domicile and, mounting upon the couch, tried to look out through one of the small

ventilators.   At first he could see nothing except that the moon and stars were obscured by
a dark cloud through which shone a dull red
glare ; but upon trying a second of the ventilators a sight was revealed that froze his blood
with horror.   The summit of the mountain
was all ablaze with the mighty fires of a great
volcano in full eruption.   Clouds of vapour and
ashes rose and spread themselves across the
heavens, while now and again the detonation
of some explosion of pent-up lava rolled
toward him, to be followed by the blaring of
the trumpets from the direction of the temple
and the wailings of the crowd in the city
square.

Upon Vance's mind, dazed at first by an
imperfect realisation of the catastrophe, was
gradually forced an overmastering sense of the
frightful fatality that seemed to pursue him.
A volcano that had rested for many years and
which there had seemed fair reason to hope
might now be extinct had broken forth with
terrific violence at the very moment when its
activity was fraught with results of which he
dared not think.   For a few moments he was

oppressed by a feeling of almost superstitious dread and he found himself wondering whether the beings of barbarous demonologies might not, after all, have existence and be vested by God with some mysterious powers for evil.

But soon a new commotion of sounds came to his ears. It was the measured clashing of cymbals and the tramp of marching men. Nearer it drew and nearer, until Vance, maddened by the terrible situation, forgetful of the dead priest, and heedless of whatever risks his action might entail upon him, hurried to the door and pushed his way out into the crowd.

For a while, absorbed as they were in what they saw in the distance, few seemed to notice the man who, bareheaded and with wild eyes, elbowed his way among them. Then they began to draw back from around him, whispering to each other and pointing out his whereabouts to those who were behind. There did not seem to be much of hostility in their attitude, but rather something akin to that awed interest with which spectators view a criminal on his way to execution.

Scarcely had Vance, in the disturbed state

of his mind, become conscious of the diversion
of public interest which his appearance had
occasioned, when the dense mass before him
opened to right and left, and he saw advancing from the direction of the great temple, a
long procession of priests.   In front was Aroo
himself.   Then came his companions, marching four abreast.   Far to the rear the cymbals
of the musicians marked time for the priestly
marchers, while over all the light of a thousand
torches flashed and played.

Involuntarily the American drew himself to
one side.   He was now almost in front of the
entrance of the palace, and, as the head of the
column drew near to where he stood, he caught
the eyes of the high-priest fixed upon him with
an expression which could mean nothing but
malignant hatred and the consciousness of
triumph.   It was only for an instant, and then
Aroo turned and began to ascend the broad
steps, followed by his grim cohorts.

At that moment Vance felt a sharp pull at
his sleeve, and, wheeling quickly, saw Nhar,
with his eyes apparently absorbed in watching
the passing procession and his finger at his

lips as if to forbid questioning or even recognition. Perceiving that he was observed, the
boy turned away in seeming carelessness, but
as his gaze crossed Vance's face it carried with
it a decided meaning. Then he commenced
to work his way back through the crowd and
the American followed with such speed as
caution permitted, for he had now recovered
something of his self-control and began to feel
that false calmness which often comes from
the magnitude of an emergency so great as to
benumb nervousness itself, just as the shock of
the most serious physical injuries sometimes
deadens the pain.

Thus, making fair headway among people
who were too deeply absorbed in what was
occurring to observe whether they were jostled
or not, the two soon found themselves at the
edge of the square, from which point Nhar,
plunging into a side street, quickened his pace
and finally broke into a run. Vance followed
and saw the other dart into a small house
which he recognised as the one where he had
left Lirrhi on the previous evening. In a moment the American had also entered and found

the priest sitting up, supported by cushions, and with a feverish excitement burning in his dark eyes.

" Ah!" he said, " you have come. That is wise. It has happened as I feared."

" But the horrible fatality of it!" cried Vance. " Who could dream of such a mischance—now—before some plan could be devised—— "

He stopped short, for the priest's face wore an expression so peculiar as to check at once the trend of his thoughts and direct them in some new channel, the line of which, however, he tried vainly to make out.

" What is it ?" he asked helplessly, after a short silence. " What do you mean ?"

Lirrhi did not seem to hear the questions. " They tell me," he said, " that Tao is angry and that Aroo has gone to the Soveet to demand the sacrifice."

" Now ? At once ?" cried Vance, springing to his feet.

" There will be little delay, as there has been little," replied Lirrhi gloomily. They fear your presence. That is evident."

Goaded to madness by a sudden realisation
of his utter impotence, Vance waited to hear
no more. One idea dominated all others,—
to rush into the royal presence, shoot down
his arch-enemy, and be killed, after slaying as
many of the fiend-priests as his revolvers and
sword would suffice for. Without heeding the
cries of Lirrhi or Nhar's attempt to restrain
him, he burst out into the street again and
commenced a mad race back to the square.

Vaguely conscious that someone was pursuing him, he redoubled his efforts, and, reaching the outskirts of the crowd, drove into them
as a ship under full sail cleaves the ocean in
her path. Angry faces, fierce threats, even
drawn swords, were in his wake; but the violence that called them into being soon left them
far behind and confined by a fast-closing barrier
of men that blocked the chance of pursuit.
So, buffeting his way, he at last gained the
steps, panting and breathless, his clothing torn
almost to shreds, but grasping tightly the
weapons upon which he depended for his final
act of vengeance.

The last of the priests had disappeared, but

the musicians remained without in a solid body and, having turned about, were facing the crowd. Their dismal music still droned fitfully as if to maintain and strengthen the spirit of depression which possessed the people.

Without attempting to burst through their ranks, Vance bounded up the steps and, turning to one side, skirted the dense array. They viewed him lazily, with more of wonder than any other sentiment, and made no effort whatever to prevent the wild - looking, half - clad man from entering the palace. A moment more and he found himself in the great court where he and his shipmates had lately been banqueted.

A strange scene lay before him. At the farthest end of the enclosure he could see, by the fitful gleam of the torches, Merrak seated upon a low throne, his chin resting upon his hand. Behind and on either side of him was ranged a close array of the nobility, brilliant with their snowy tunics and scarlet cloaks, while, in sharp contrast of colours, the entire court, up almost to the Soveet's footstool, was packed with a dense mass of black mantles and dark faces. All the priesthood of the island seemed to be gathered together, but not a sound came from the great multitude except the voice of one man, speaking in low, measured tones.

Vance raised himself a little by the aid of the base of a column, so as to see over the heads of those before him, and made out with some difficulty that the voice came from a small cleared space directly in front of the throne and occupied by a single individual. A second glance told him that it was Aroo himself. Then he dropped to the floor again and began to push his way toward the spot where he knew the fatal words were being uttered.

In a few moments, he scarce knew how, he had gained the front of the circle that enclosed the high-priest. The commotion occasioned by his approach had not escaped the latter's attention and, as the foreigner burst through the last line, Aroo turned and regarded him fixedly for a moment. Then he faced the Soveet again and went on with his speech.

Amid all his excitement, Vance could not

but note and marvel at the strange forbearance with which his furious intrusion had been received by a vast concourse of armed men every one of whom he recognised by a hundred signs to be his deadly enemy. Sobered for an instant by this thought, utterly exhausted by his terrible efforts, and feeling secure for the moment in what seemed the contempt of his foes, he forbore to accomplish his purpose at once. He reasoned grimly that his hand would be much steadier and surer when his strength and wind returned. So he stood and listened to the words of the high-priest of Tao, to whom his own arrival seemed to have furnished a new theme.

" It is not strange,'' continued that worthy, " that Tao is angry with his people, for have they not listened to the impious words of the stranger, who thinks to subvert all things to the measure of his wishes ? And have not even you, O Prince, given heed in your heart to the thought that Tao should relinquish the bride which the years bring to him ? Not long since my blood boiled within me at the thought of the insult, and I was then minded to ask the

life of the stranger.   But Tao is a god that
enforces his own rights and I now see clearly
that it is not his will that the ignorance of any
man should bring him to everlasting blackness.
Therefore it is ordered that this fellow should
live to see her to whom he would so vainly as-
pire given unto the ruler of the universe, who
has been pleased to dwell among and bless us
who have ever revered and served him.

  " Let my lord now give the word that the
nuptials of the maid, his daughter, be solem-
nised according to the ancient rites.   Speak,
honoured one of Tao!   Behold now the flaming crown that rests upon the god's brow and
threatens to consume all worlds that honour
him not."

  As he finished speaking, he pointed toward
the mountain-top, clearly visible from that part
of the court.   The eyes of the Soveet followed
his finger and rested for a moment upon the
lurid coronet gleaming through the night and
through the volumes of smoke and vapour that
encumbered the atmosphere even where they
stood.   Vance saw the Prince shudder slightly
as his glance fell again upon the stern, cruel

face of the priest.   Several times he gathered himself as if to speak, but his voice would not answer his bidding.   His face was drawn with an expression of intense anguish.   The trumpets and cymbals had ceased their clamour. Even the mountain flamed in silence, and Vance almost imagined that he could hear the fall of the flakes of white ashes descending in an endless cloud upon their heads.

A sudden consciousness of the absurdity and ignorance of it all flashed through his mind. Surely these people were sufficiently enlightened to be able to understand the truth about such phenomena.   Moved by an impulse born of this idea, and perhaps with the thought that it would be better to provoke violence than to begin by shooting men down in cold blood, he stepped forward into the open space, and, fixing his eyes upon the Soveet, said:

" Will you permit me to speak ? "

The stricken ruler did not answer. He looked wonderingly, almost vacantly, at the strange figure before him.   Aroo turned quickly at the sound of the new voice and took a step toward the interloper.   Then a smile of contemptuous malice curled his lips and he made no effort at interruption.

"Can it be," pursued Vance, speaking rapidly and heedless of the many blunders and the rude accent which caused some of his enemies to laugh outright, "that a people dwelling with nature are ignorant of the causes which make mountains burst forth with flame and smoke and lava, as does yours now ? Do you not know how the gases, generated deep in the earth, break from their prison-houses time and again and find vent through many such cratered summits in all parts of the world, and that men call these volcanoes ? I myself have seen as many as fifty. Surely you would not hold all to be the abodes of gods ?" He stopped, for it was not difficult to note the spirit with which his words were received. Among the priests they excited an animosity which bade fair to effect his secondary purpose and which the restraining voice and hand of Aroo seemed hardly able to hold in check. The face of that potentate was inscrutable. As for the nobles who flanked the throne, some gazed upon the speaker with contempt, some with pity for what they evidently considered the unbalanced state of his mind. Even he himself was conscious how feeble his statements must sound to his auditors.

Still they served to rouse the Soveet from the condition of apparent collapse into which he had sunk.

" Why did you not remain in the house which I assigned to you ? " he said sternly. " I have borne much from your disregard of my wishes and my warnings. It is your action that has brought the anger of Tao himself upon me and my people and has torn from me my child, who might yet (for I have ever honoured and obeyed the god and his sons) have comforted many years of my life and perhaps even been spared to its end and escaped the accursed honour that hangs over her race. You, on the other hand, suffer nothing you have not yourself invited. Do you dream we could be fools enough to believe it to be insensate nature that menaces with a danger that experience has often shown is abated at once by the sacrifice which my

people now demand ?   Is nature amenable to
such a measure ?   You speak whereof you know
nothing.   Would I had slain you when your
life was first demanded by him who now pro-
tects you from me,—even the favourite son of
Tao whom you never cease to blaspheme."

Then, turning to the high-priest, he continued in a firm voice: " Son of Tao, I, the
Soveet, have heard your words and, as the law
and my people demand, I accept in my own
name and in the name of the most happy
virgin my daughter the offer of marriage you
have borne to me this day.   May she find
favour for herself and for us all in the eyes of
her lord and husband, and may he pardon the
breast of a father who relinquishes his off-
spring with tears — even to this, the most
exalted of fates.   Let my lord Aroo and the
proper officers take measures that the usual
ceremonies be duly observed.   It is decreed."

He sank back in his seat and made a motion
as if to draw his mantle over his face.   Vance's
teeth were clenched and he saw nothing of the
scene that whirled around him.   He clutched
his revolver tightly while he strove to brush

aside the cloud that obscured his vision and bade fair to obstruct his aim.   At that moment he felt his wrist firmly grasped and a hand laid over his mouth.

CHAPTER XV

A CONFLICT OF AUTHORITY

IT would have been difficult for Vance to understand, much less explain, the strange calm which came over him at this first touch of restraint. The interruption seemed to dispel at once every impulse that was dragging him toward the suicidal act upon which his mind had been set, and now, without opposition, without even recognising the agency, he suffered himself to be drawn away to one side; and when he had regained a consciousness of his surroundings it was to find himself being hurried through the deserted streets of the city. Then gradually, but still without the aid of his rapidly clearing eyesight, he began to realise that the hand which gripped his wrist was that of Nhar. All volition on his own part seemed to be suspended, but his

thoughts were free and active, nor were they
of a nature to afford him even reasonable satisfaction. He had never in past years had
reason to believe himself a man of weak character, and yet he could not but admit that in
the present emergency he had acted like the
veriest child,—headstrong, yet led by every
foolish impulse when left to himself, and, on
the other hand, ready to give up his purpose
and fall under the influence of a mere boy
whenever that influence was exerted by touch
or even presence. He was beginning to enter-
tain an almost superstitious dread of these
dark islanders, whose impassive faces seemed
to hide such mysterious powers, and he ceased
to wonder that the descendants of the Carthaginian fugitives, with all their superiority
of knowledge and equipment, had in time
fallen so completely under the sway of an inferior race. Nothing but a consciousness of
the most absolute power, he reasoned, could
have impelled Aroo to treat him with the personal forbearance which he had now experienced more than once, while the control which
savages like Lirrhi and Nhar exercised over

him, an officer of the American navy and a man of cultivated mind and broad experience, seemed explicable only on the score of occultism or at least mesmeric influence. These thoughts, added to his sense of absolute helplessness and dependence, were in no wise calculated to foster conceit, and therefore it was that he arrived at Lirrhi's house with feelings very much akin to those of a disobedient child detected in some act for which punishment is impending.

In such a frame of mind he entered, but there was no look of reproof in the priest's face. This, too, was in a sense humiliating. It seemed to show that he also regarded Vance as a child whose lapses of obedience or good judgment were to be expected and condoned; and to be so regarded by another was much worse than to admit the fact to one's self.

Without a word as to this latest and very broad breach of their agreement, Lirrhi pointed to a veiled figure standing in the shadow at the rear of the room, and said:

" This woman wishes to speak with you. I sent Nhar to bring you to her."

13

Vance's heart leaped as his eye fell upon the visitor, but at that instant she threw her veil aside and he saw that it was the elder of the maids who had attended him on the first night he had spent in the Soveet's palace. She seemed now much agitated and somewhat distrustful of those around her, for, beckoning rather imperiously to the American, she drew him to the farthest corner of the room and began speaking in a low tone but very rapidly, as though fearful of forgetting her message:

" My mistress sent me to tell you three things: that she loves you alone and always; that she commands you to make no effort to save her, which she knows to be hopeless, but, on the other hand, adjures you to use every endeavour to escape from this place; and, third, that I give you her farewell for all time, unless— " and the woman seemed to hesitate for a moment—" unless, in some future life, your God shall be more powerful than Tao, our master, and you can persuade Him to kill the devourer of virgins and release those whom he holds in thrall. That hope she bids me tell you to keep as your only one."

In a moment she had drawn her cloak about her face again and darted out. Vance sprang forward, bent upon compelling some further speech or at least sending a return message; but the voice of Lirrhi, raised in such a tone of absolute command as he had never heard in it before, compelled him to halt in his tracks.

" What new foolishness were you bent upon now ? " said the priest.

Vance's brain was clear enough to note the assurance of power conveyed by the past tense of the verb.

" To send back word that I love her and will save her or die also," he said, as he stood hesitating between obedience and rebellion.

" Are all white men as silly as your people and our men from the sea ? " murmured the other wearily. " Come near now and listen to the wisdom of dark races. It is but lovers' folly, for which there is no time, to say that you love her. She knows that you have re-mained here at much peril, and she knows that it is for that reason alone. As for your other message, it can but further disturb her with fears for your safety without bringing any hope of success. Why is it that white men seem always anxious to defeat their own ends ? "

" What end have I to look to except the end of my life ? " said Vance, gloomily, as he sank upon a low stool. Then he sprang to his feet again. " Will you tell me," he asked, " whether there is any good reason now why I should not force my way through them and see her and speak to her ? "

" Be patient. You would be cut down before you had gained a tenth of the way. Do not dream that the forbearance of the priests will last always; and remember that even the people themselves are ready to tear you to pieces, for they look upon you as the cause of all their troubles and those of their ruler,—as an enemy of their god."

" And an enemy of their fiend-god I am," interrupted Vance, quickly,—" one that has forces at command of which they and you know nothing; who carries the lives of ten men at his belt. If white men are fools, they at least know secrets of war that to the peoples who depend upon sword and spear seem miracles of thunder and lightning and death."

The eyes of Lirrhi flashed with a sudden gleam of satisfaction, but he showed little curiosity.

" If that be so," he said, " save your magic for the time when it may avail."

" They shall avail me now, at least to see her," cried Vance. " As for being killed myself, I imagine that 's pretty definitely down on the programme, is n't it ? "

He moved toward the door. Nhar was crouching in a corner with head sunken upon his breast and body rocking slowly to and fro. Lirrhi bent his dark eyes fixedly upon the recalcitrant.

" Would you rather see her and die or save her and perchance live ? " he said slowly.

" Tell me how, then, in God's name ! " exclaimed the American, turning quickly and approaching the couch. " You treat me as a child ; you tell me nothing of your plans and yet expect me to rely upon them and remain idle when every hope seems to have slipped away before my eyes."

" I treat you as a child because you are a child," said Lirrhi sternly ; " and those who would be trusted must show themselves worthy of trust. If you have measures of your own that promise success, I shall not hinder you from pursuing them; for it is no small thing that a priest of my race should be false to his god and his brothers. I have risked much for you and I am ready to risk more. My life is already in the cast, but I owe to you more than life, and we pay our debts. I will tell you nothing. Trust me or not, as you choose; but if you trust you must obey or I shall fall with you and to no purpose,—which would be as unwise as are your actions."

Vance again felt himself wavering under the strength of this strange man. The rather scornful question as to his own plans was one well calculated to bring him to his senses. Lirrhi might be a miracle of treachery, he reasoned, bent upon playing his benefactor false in the interest of his caste, but, even were this so, nothing could be lost by waiting a day longer before consummating a purpose which looked only to revenge and perhaps a word and a pressure of the hand to be pur- chased at the price of self-annihilation. It was, however, with little confidence in the result that he yielded.

" Will you not even tell me how soon we shall strike ? " he asked, seating himself again.

The priest seemed busy with his thoughts. When he answered his voice was softer.

" The time may be soon, but not until they take the maiden to the nuptial house of Tao. Then, if you are as brave and strong as you are heedless and wilful, we shall strike, and I shall pay my debt. I had hoped to delay as long as might be, in order that my own strength should be restored and fortified the more,—for the task is no light one."

" You are right and I am a fool," cried Vance. " A sane man would not need to be told that he could rescue a woman more readily from a solitary hut in the woods than from a crowded city. We shall go there the first night, then ? "

" No," said Lirrhi, with a touch of impatience in his tones, " unless you still wish to fail and die. Do you think Aroo also is bereft of reason ? There will be thirty armed priests watching day and night around the house, and others not far away, until——"

" We shall have a chance even against that number," said Vance. He was once more calm and deliberate,—even a little ashamed of his late outbreak.

" Do you accept my terms ?" said Lirrhi, without heeding the interruption. " Remember, Aroo will not be there, and while he lives you can hope for no safety, even should you kill or put to flight all the guards."

" And you will at least help me to kill him if we fail ?"

" Wicked men fall sometimes into their own snares," replied the priest evasively.

" Well, I will obey your commands," said Vance, after a short pause ; " if you are ready to trust me again when I tell you all I have done." And in a few words he narrated the adventure of the preceding night.

" You did both ill and well," said Lirrhi, " ill to admit Mapo, and doubly ill to go with him ; well to refuse his treacherous offer, and doubly well to kill him. I will take care that the body be safely disposed of. And now it

is wise that you should exchange your torn
garments for clothes that are less strange.
Nhar will give you a priest's robe and tunic
and stain your face and hands and feet. You
shall remain here, too, and sleep in the loft.
Aroo does not wish you to be killed—yet. He
hates you too much for that; but doubtless
many of the people are thirsty for your blood,
and since your foolish action of to-night caution is doubly necessary.''

Unable to question the very manifest wisdom
of this suggestion, Vance followed the boy up a
ladder through a trap-door and into a low loft,
where he was soon transformed by deft fingers
into a very fair semblance of a minister of that
cult against the whole power of which they
three were to pit their slender strength. His
moustache and the front of his head were
closely shaven, but he took care to buckle his
pistol-belt under the long tunic which fell
over and concealed the weapons. His sword,
too, he could not bring himself to exchange
for the short, serpentine blade befitting his new
character, so the plan was finally devised of
swinging it over his shoulder, where it hung

down his back, hidden by the black cloak. The native sword was bound at his side over the pistols, and Nhar, stepping back, surveyed the result of his labours with as much satisfaction as the dim lamplight would permit.   Then he disclosed a small store of provisions and a jar of water which he had brought with him, placed them near the pile of old garments that were evidently intended to serve as a bed and, with a parting injunction that Vance should remain there and be silent until notified that it was time to act, extinguished the lamp and descended into the room below, closing the trap-door behind him.

CHAPTER XVI

THE BEGINNING

LEFT to his own thoughts, the prisoner began first to speculate as to how far the night was advanced. At last he fell asleep, and awoke to transfer his speculations to the day. This proved a more solvable problem, for, by the increasing dimness of certain shreds of light that lay near cracks under the eaves, he judged that the sun must be already low, and then he watched them for hours and hours, as it seemed to him, before they had entirely faded out. After that he lay and listened to the sounds of never-ceasing activity that rang through the city. Several times he realised that large bodies of men were marching through streets not far distant, for the tramp of moving feet, mingled with words of command, interrupted the blare of trumpets and

clash of cymbals that came almost constantly
to his ears from the direction of the great
square.   Finally, however, all the noises began to die slowly away, still sounding from
time to time, but as if from a greater and
greater distance, until the night seemed to
swallow them up.

Suddenly it flashed through his mind that
the priests were most probably now escorting
their victim to the place of sacrifice.   That
explained all.   With a strong effort he crushed
down the spirit of insubordination which had
again begun to assert itself.   He remembered
that by what was evidently intended as a re-
finement of cruelty, but most fortunately in
the present instance, food sufficient to sustain
life for several days was placed in the living
tomb, and that, apart from the agony of mind
connected with such a situation, no physical
suffering need be apprehended for a considerable time.   Cheered somewhat by this reflection, he comforted himself as well as he could
and, toward morning, sank again into a
troubled sleep.

How long he slept there was no means of

knowing, but gradually he became conscious of a strange, monotonous sound droning in his ears. At first he tried to ignore it and go to sleep once more, but, in spite of all his efforts, his faculties seemed gradually sharpened to almost abnormal acuteness.

The vague noise resolved itself into the unmistakable groaning of a human voice, evidently of some one in deep agony. Vance struggled to speak, to ask the name of the sufferer and how he had come or been brought to his hiding-place, but the words would not form themselves. Then he imagined that Lirrhi was dying in the room below; perhaps he had been attacked and wounded by assassins. He determined that he must descend to help him; for if the priest died, all hope would be indeed gone; and yet the effort to move proved as vain as the effort to speak.

And now a sudden glare of light illumined the loft,—not the light of day but the yellow gleam of fire. He could make out a figure writhing and tossing upon the floor near the trap-door through which he had entered, and the figure was unmistakably a woman's.

Dumfounded at such an apparition, his mind was groping blindly to explain her presence, when she slowly rose and tottered toward him, and he recognised, clad in gorgeous robes of scarlet and gold and decked with unnumbered jewels that flashed weirdly, the Princess Zelkah. Then, as his eyes dwelt for a moment on her features, he turned and, burying his head among the stuff upon which he lay, burst into a paroxysm of tears and sobs. The face he had seen was drawn with an emaciation that could indicate only the presence of death; the cheeks and jaws seemed bursting through the yellow skin, while the eyes had dilated until they appeared almost larger than the head itself. The figure, too, matched well with the terrors of the face, for the rich garments hung upon it as upon a skeleton. A breath as of famine was wafted to his nostrils, and at last his mind sprang to a realisation of the truth. Lirrhi had been guilty of the blackest treachery. Some drug had been mingled with his food or drink, and days— perhaps weeks—had passed as a few hours. She was dead, and now her spirit had come to

arouse him and to call for revenge upon the
fiends who had wrought all this wickedness
and woe. He strove to rise, but at that moment he felt his arms pinioned to his sides, and
distinguished the face of Aroo himself within
a few inches of his own, the eyes glaring into
his with an expression of unquenchable hate.

Gathering all his powers for one final effort,
he clinched furiously with his adversary, while
the sorrowful shade stood near, silent, gazing
at the combat. Suddenly both seemed to disappear. He found himself with his arms free,
half kneeling upon the tossed and tumbled pile
of material that had composed his couch; and
then awakening consciousness told him that
all, the vision and the grapple, had been but
the phantasms of a dream which his troubled
mind had called into being. It was many
minutes, however, before he could convince
himself of this, so real were all the terrible
details, and so complete the physical exhaustion that had supervened. He shuddered at
the recollection; but at last his mind grew
clearer, the mist of sleep became entirely
dissipated and he noticed from the light

streaming through the cracks that the day must be far advanced.

And now a new anxiety began to molest him. Why had not some word come from Lirrhi ? In spite of his knowledge that the experiences of the last few minutes had been a dream, he was beginning to find himself attaching almost an occult import to whatever occurred in this strange land. How far the effect was strengthened in the present instance by the certainty, born of the evidences of the past night, that Zelkah was already confined in that awful chamber, would have been difficult to determine, but his growing impatience was on the point of asserting itself to the extent of once more provoking him to break his parole and to descend into the room below for at least new information.

It was a fortunate chance that he experienced some difficulty, in the half-darkness, in finding the trap-door through which he had entered; for, as he felt carefully around, there came to his ears the unmistakable sound of voices in conversation beneath him. He ceased searching for the movable boards, and, putting

his ear close to the floor, listened eagerly.
There could be no possible doubt that several
persons were below, and, while their words
were indistinguishable, he recognised one voice
as that of Lirrhi and that it was raised in protest.   Then another person, who certainly was
not Nhar, replied in lower, deeper tones that
thrilled through him indescribably, and again
Lirrhi exclaimed, this time louder and more
clearly, as if he wished the words to reach
Vance's ears:

"I do not know why you thought me
cognisant of his whereabouts. Have you examined the house which the Soveet assigned
him ?"

Once more the answer was too low to be
caught by the listener, but Lirrhi's next speech
disclosed its import:

"Then rest assured that some of our people
have made away with him in their anger";
and later, in reply to a further murmur of the
visitor's, he said, "Doubtless the priests
would obey you, but the people are incensed
past endurance. They know nothing of your
deeper schemes for vengeance. Perhaps even

this absence of Mapo may be in some way connected with the foreigner's disappearance."

The conversation then sank into lower tones
and finally ceased altogether, but to the fugitive it had been significant in many ways. It
removed whatever doubt he might have had
as to the good faith of Lirrhi, and made him
more willing to abide by the plans devised by
the priest. There was no reasonable question
in his mind but that the other speaker had
been either Aroo or some emissary sent by him
to discover Vance's whereabouts, and it was
perfectly evident that Lirrhi, in dispelling
whatever suspicions the visitor might have
entertained, had committed himself very
deeply. Therefore the fugitive awaited the
outcome with more patience and confidence
than he had yet felt, while he winced to think
what the result might have been had he succeeded in his attempt to descend.

Hour after hour dragged along wearily
enough and by the time the light between the
crevices again began to grow dim, indicating
the approach of another night, his nerves, if
not his doubts, were once more active.

Scarcely, however, had utter darkness set in, when he was startled by a fumbling at the trap-door, and the sound of a bolt sliding back told him that his friends had not relied so entirely upon his prudence as to neglect more substantial precautions.   He was not in a mood to harbour the momentary feeling of irritation aroused by this evidence that they still regarded him very much as an unruly boy, and he almost smiled when his common sense forced him to admit, on second thought, that such an attitude was quite justifiable.

In a moment the boards rose slowly and a head appeared from below.   The words " Descend now, and be silent," came to his ears in a whisper; then,—" It is I, Nahr."

Hastily Vance followed the boy down the ladder, having first assured himself that his weapons were both concealed and readily available.   A single lamp lighted the lower room, but it was several minutes before his eyes became accustomed even to that.   Then he saw Lirrhi standing erect with his sword and dagger thrust in his belt.   Nhar also was fully armed and carried, in addition to his weapons,

several short torches made of wood smeared
with some resinous substance.   It was evident
that the time for action had at last arrived, and
Vance's heart leaped at the thought that he
would now be able to strike a blow for his
own cause and show that he was not altogether a child to be patronised and guided
and restrained.

A feeling, however, of concern crossed his
mind as to the ability of Lirrhi to take part in
such an expedition as seemed to have been
projected.

" But your hurt ? " he asked, looking
anxiously at the priest.   " Can you go with
us without danger ? "

The thin lips curled slightly.

" Your race is a strange one," he said.
" When others hold back you would rush forward, and when they are ready you hold back.
We, on the other hand, follow a purpose once
resolved upon.   When it is time to do a thing
we are able to do it.   No, I shall not go without danger, but I shall run no more risk than
you do,—perhaps not as much, for there are
many men to be killed, and I shall not be able

to help you in that way, as I might if entirely whole.''

He raised his mantle, and Vance saw that he was wrapped in a network of crossed bandages as skilfully applied as if by the most accomplished surgeon.

'' We live frugally and are hardy and healthy,'' he added, reassuringly, '' and my bones will knit in half the time it would take a white man's. In two days more I should have been well, but, as it is, you will not find me far behind you, in endurance at least. If I be not as forward in the fighting, you may thank your own impatience for it.''

For a moment Vance found himself wondering which he would rather face,—the cunning and malignant enmity of Aroo or the patronising, superior friendship of Lirrhi. Then he recalled a statement Deshon had once made as to the remarkable readiness to heal noticed in the wounds of animals and certain savage races, as though it were a special provision of nature to compensate for their lack of the knowledge and the means for artificial treatment. All such thoughts, however, were rapidly driven away by the grim joy that came to him with the news that there was fighting to be done.

At a word from Lirrhi the lamp was extinguished by Nahr, who then opened the door cautiously and, after looking up and down the street, motioned for the others to come out. As the priest left the room, Vance saw that he carried in his hand a wooden tablet, about a foot square, inscribed with Phœnician characters and provided with a hook at the top.

CHAPTER XVII

THE FIRST BLOW

THE night was dark, devoid of moon or stars. Only the glare of the volcano illumined all the western heavens, while the cloud of fine white ashes still hung over the city and descended slowly, until it had now covered the streets to the depth of an inch or more with its sepulchral cloak.

Lirrhi, followed by his two companions, turned his steps toward the great square. From time to time men passed them, but the spectacle of two priests with an attendant was not one to excite comment, and Vance congratulated himself upon the wisdom and completeness of his disguise.

At length they reached the square and, crossing it, approached the palace.

There the Lieutenant noticed, for the first

time, along the side nearest the temple, a row of low posts on several of which tablets were hanging like that which Lirrhi had brought with him. The characters with which these were inscribed were, of course, undecipherable in the darkness. Lirrhi at once proceeded to affix his to one of the unoccupied posts, and then, without vouchsafing any explanation, turned aside and, passing close by the temple, led the way in the direction of the mountain.

Vance had not been enough interested in the posts and the pendent tablets to ask any questions. He was too eager to get at the real work that lay before them, and now, as they hurried through the gate and, leaving walls and houses behind them, struck out along the broad, well-paved road that led to the sacred ground, his blood began to course more swiftly through his veins, and his step and carriage bore witness that he felt himself free at last from the irksome bonds of absolute subordination to which his peculiar position had compelled him to submit. The consciousness that he had badly needed these same bonds did not help to make them more grateful, — which is an unreasonable and unpraiseworthy attribute of human nature.

For upwards of half an hour they followed the road by which they had returned to the city. Then, after they had halted long enough to gird up their tunics to the knee, Lirrhi struck off along an almost imperceptible wood-path which branched to the right and seemed to lead through the densest thickets and toward the wildest and least inhabited part of the island. Nothing was visible in the darkness. The undergrowth was too heavy to permit of carrying a lighted torch, and Nhar was even compelled to kneel from time to time, to make sure they had not wandered from their way. As for Vance, he soon lost all idea of locality, and it was only when his foot struck against a broad, flat stone that he divined they had at last reached the border of the sacred ground.

As they began the ascent, circling the mountain in the opposite direction to that followed by Nhar when leading him to his first place of concealment, the full terrors of the eruption became apparent. The thinning branches and foliage no longer obscured the sky, now all aglow with the light which seemed doubly brilliant against the lurid background of smoke and vapour.   Explosions followed one another in quick succession and at each outburst a great pillar of fire shot up many hundred feet. He could even hear the molten streams of lava forcing their way down the steep decline and leaping in cascades of flame over the precipices that lay in their paths.

The course which the party had chosen was free from this source of danger, the only menace to their safety being the fall, from time to time, of huge stones that, hurled upward by the explosion of the subterranean gases, came crashing back through trees and bushes, and sometimes, unless buried in the earth by the force of their descent, bounded away down the mountain-side, carrying ruin and desolation.   Vance soon concluded that he could quite pardon the natives for their dislike of himself, if they deemed him in any way responsible for the horror that enveloped their island; his only wonder was at the forbearance of a people so barbarous as to believe in such

an agency and so cruel as to seek to stay it by
so terrible a means as the one employed.

The three had halted several times to allow
Lirrhi to rest, for almost at the foot of the
mountain the visible path had ceased, and
their way, which now lay over rough, uneven
ground, was indicated by landmarks indistinguishable by any but the priest. Even he fre-
quently found difficulty in locating some point
in the darkness, and such work was of necessity
exhausting to a man who had just risen from
his bed and whose broken bones could at the
best be but feebly knit.

The first part of the journey was, however,
nearly over. Lirrhi climbed more slowly,
stopping every few steps to examine trees and
rocks with the most minute attention. At
last he halted beneath a smooth, vine-covered
ledge about half-way up the ascent. Nhar
glanced inquiringly toward him and then, in
answer to an almost imperceptible nod, proceeded to draw the vines aside here and there,
until finally, at the base of the rock, he disclosed a small circular orifice about two feet
in diameter and evidently of artificial origin.

Then, at another nod from the priest, the boy got down upon his hands and knees and proceeded to crawl through the aperture. Lirrhi promptly followed, motioning to Vance to do likewise. In a few moments they stood upright, but in absolute darkness.

The priest now directed Nhar to light one of his torches. By its glare, Vance made out that they were standing in a narrow ravine about two feet wide, with smooth perpendicular sides of lava rock rising to a height of nearly ten feet. The top was covered with what seemed a thick network of vines, and the pathway was of solid lava carefully and laboriously levelled and evened off by human agency; in fact, all the surroundings impressed the American with the idea of man's workmanship. The passage was practically undiscoverable unless one should fall through some break in the vines that roofed it, and, in this connection, it crossed his mind that the ravine where he had found Lirrhi might have been originally devoted to similar purposes — whatever these might be — until the ground above had caved in through some agitation connected with the

volcanic phenomena that dominated nature in
this mysterious region.

His thoughts were, however, quickly interrupted by a sharp whisper of Lirrhi's. Nhar
at once extinguished his torch, and both
seemed to listen intently. For a moment
Vance could not detect the sound to which
their more acute hearing was evidently keenly
alive. Then he, too, caught the unmistakable
fall of footsteps upon the lava, and soon a dim
light, which gradually became brighter and
brighter, seemed to pervade the dense gloom
before them.

A few feet farther on, the path took a sharp
turn, and beyond this the footfalls of the
torch-bearer were now rapidly approaching.
Lirrhi clutched Vance's arm.

"Your sword," he whispered sharply.
"Go close to the turn, and use it surely.
There is but one of them."

Vance shuddered.

"Kill a man like that?" he murmured.
"We call that murder."

"Call it what you please—afterward," said
Lirrhi impatiently, "but do not speak now.

If he escapes, we and the girl are dead.   That is all; and, remember, it is a priest, and one very close to her misfortunes.''

Vance hesitated no longer, but, swinging his sword around from his back to his side, he drew it carefully from the scabbard and advanced to the point where the path turned. The next moment a priest bearing a flambeau stood within two feet of him and he felt himself lunging with all his strength straight at the man's heart.

The harsh, grating sound of steel piercing through flesh and bone came to his ears and, with it, a short, stifled cry, beginning in surprise and running the gamut of terror and pain.   The torch fell and was extinguished. He was conscious of wrenching his sword loose and thrusting again even while his enemy was falling; but the first stroke had been true and the priest uttered no further sound.

Trembling, and streaming with perspiration, the slayer stepped quickly over the body and hurried around the curve that he might not see the corpse of the only man he had ever killed outside of fair fight.   Nhar and Lirrhi

had now come forward, and the former proceeded to relight his torch while the latter
knelt down and satisfied himself that the
victim was really dead.   Then they followed
Vance to where he stood trying to realise
whether his present feelings were like those
that beset common murderers.

" There are eleven more," said Lirrhi, as he
overtook the Lieutenant, and Vance shuddered
again at the ominous words.   He found himself going so far as to hope that the rest of
their enemies might be killed while defending
themselves, even though victory should be im-
perilled by allowing them such an opportunity.

They pushed on very rapidly now along the
ravine, that turned and twisted every few feet
as though writhing in pain.   At one point the
light of Nhar's torch fell full upon Vance, who
glanced involuntarily down at the great gout
of blood that he knew disfigured his tunic.
Yes, there it was, but showing less clearly
against the red cloth than he had dreaded it
would.   It only glistened a little now, because
it was wet.   Soon it would dry and become
black and caked and perhaps scale off in part.

So his mind dwelt upon every scrap of minute detail that suggested itself, and wandered off into musings as to the probable reflections of a man to be hanged for murder, imagining himself the condemned felon.

Suddenly he stopped short in his progress. He had come face to face with a smooth wall of rock that transformed the path into a perfect *cul-de-sac.* The torch that Nhar was carrying close behind threw all its light upon the surface of this obstruction, but Vance looked in vain for any aperture through which to make good their advance.

The momentary chill that fell over him at this seeming check, which his first thought attributed to some convulsion connected with the eruption, soon gave place to returning confidence, for the face of Lirrhi showed no surprise or indecision. He stepped close to the end wall and examined it carefully, while Nhar held the torch so as to give as much light as possible.

In a moment the priest motioned to Vance and pointed to a shadow on the stone which seemed, on close inspection, to be a very slight, almost imperceptible, indentation in the shape of a human hand.

" Place your palm and fingers in the lines," he said, " and press evenly and steadily."

Vance did so, and at his second effort the result was startling. A portion of the rock several feet in height and breadth revolved slowly as on a pivot and disclosed cavernous depths beyond that seemed to lead straight into the very bowels of the mountain. Despite his excitement at this *dénouement*, he could but wonder at the nice adjustment that left not so much as a crack visible to the eye and yet permitted tons of solid rock to be moved by the mere pressure of a hand. The incident, however, served to startle him out of the morbid vein of thought which had seemed likely to cripple his energies at the very time when the call upon them was sure to be most pressing.

One by one the three entered the mountain and, after swinging the door-block — if it might so be called — nearly back to its position, pursued their way along a sinuous passage, narrow and scarcely high enough for one man to walk erect in, and with walls, floor, and ceiling cut out of solid lava. It was quite apparent to Vance, in spite of the irregularity of its course, that the general trend of their path was decidedly downward.

After they had progressed for some distance, Lirrhi, who had once more taken the lead, halted and directed Nhar again to extinguish his torch. Then he advanced more slowly, stopping from time to time. Vance could feel that the priest was listening intently for some expected sound, and the knowledge that a new and probably decisive struggle was impending served to restore all needed coolness to his nerves and steadiness to his muscles.

At last, as Lirrhi halted for the third or fourth time, the American became conscious that the intense gloom was not as densely black now as it had been a moment since. He understood at once from the former experience that there must be light ahead, and with it more enemies to be destroyed.

CHAPTER XVIII

ONE MORE

AFTER a moment of hesitation, Lirrhi drew Nhar toward him and gave him some whispered direction. Vance could barely make out the two figures close together. Then the smaller parted from the other and disappeared in the direction of the light.

The moments dragged along like hours. No suspicion of a sound broke the awful stillness which the American could liken only to death and the grave. He knew that his perceptions had already become morbidly acute, and he found himself beginning almost to realise what had always seemed incomprehensible to him,—how moles and even worms could dwell in sub-terranean passages burrowed as occasion might demand, and possess senses that would enable them to pursue their prey, escape from their enemies, and perform all the varied functions of animal life.

At last a faint sound came to his ears. Lirrhi heard it too,—the sound of approaching footsteps,—Nhar returning from his mission.

With a low warning lest he might be mistaken for an enemy, the boy glided forward like a shadow and, coming close to the priest, whispered earnestly in his ear.

" There is a large chamber a short distance along the gallery," Lirrhi repeated to Vance, in low tones. " Nhar tells me there are five men on guard there, but that two are sleeping."

" I hope there will be some fight in them," the American whispered. " Fighting is the life of killing, even more truly than competition is the life of trade."

Lirrhi made no reply; but, though unable to see his face, Vance knew instinctively that it wore a look of surprise, less at his flippancy than at the reluctance of anyone to deal with enemies in the safest, most expeditious, and most effective way.

Then, each with his hand upon the shoulder

of the one before him, they crept cautiously forward, Nhar first, then Lirrhi, and Vance bringing up the rear.

Gradually the light from the chamber ahead became clearer, as they approached, pausing every moment to listen.

" You are fortunate," whispered Lirrhi. " Usually twelve priests are on guard at such a time. I do not know why Aroo has cut down the number to six."

He raised his hand, as Vance seemed about to answer, and immediately turned and motioned Nhar to lead on again.

At last the boy stopped just before a turn of the passage. Lirrhi crawled forward and, after glancing around the corner of rock, motioned to Vance to come to his side. A weird spectacle lay before their eyes.

About twenty feet beyond was a square chamber with high, vaulted roof. Several torches, mounted in convenient niches, shed a fairly bright light over the interior, showing a dark passage opposite which evidently led farther on into the mountain. In the centre of the room was a table of heavy black wood at which were seated three priests, eating and drinking. Food and wine stood before them in abundance and they spoke to each other in low tones which, while not expressing the hearty mirth of banqueters, carried with them an impression of the deep internal satisfaction of true gourmands.   In the shadow two other figures could be made out extended at full length upon pallets of dried grass and seemingly buried in slumber.

After a short survey of the situation, Lirrhi slowly drew his sword and Nhar followed his example. The latter's blade grated slightly against its scabbard: one of the men glanced up quickly. The three watchers drew back, scarcely daring to breathe.

The priest's suspicions were not seriously aroused, however, for he did not communicate them to his companions but turned again to his refection.   Lirrhi nevertheless allowed some minutes to pass before he moved a muscle.   Then he motioned to Vance, pointing to his sword and indicating his wish by drawing one hand very slowly through the other.

The American hesitated. He felt that it
was time to use every force at his command
and that to enter into a hand-to-hand fight
with but one sound man, a boy, and an invalid
against five opponents was thrusting his comrades into altogether unnecessary peril. Then,
too, the danger and excitement of it all tended
to blunt finer feelings, and, under the circumstances, an attack from ambuscade seemed
entirely justifiable. The chances were that,
even so, there would be fair odds against them.

A look of surprise not unmingled with contempt had spread over Lirrhi's features as he
noted the American's hesitation, but, paying
no attention to its import, Vance drew one of
his revolvers from his belt and, motioning his
companions aside, glided forward. They eyed
him and his weapon with astonishment. In a
moment he had stepped out into the passage
and, levelling the revolver full at the priest
who had been the most vigilant, fired.

It would have been hard to imagine the terrible effect of the detonation, that rang and
rang again as if through miles and miles of
galleries, — now almost dying out, only to

gather volume once more and roll back to their deafened ears. The smoke hung like a pall around the assailant, but he sprang through it and fired again.

The man he had aimed at had fallen at the first discharge and lay still. Another fell at the second, but almost immediately staggered to his feet again, when a third shot stretched him on the rocky floor.

Still the American continued to advance into the room, endeavouring as he did so to see through the smoke. He fired at what he took to be the form of the third feaster still sitting at his place and apparently paralysed with fear. Whether struck or not, the shot seemed to release the fellow from his bonds, for he sprang up with a yell and, as if blinded, rushed straight toward his enemy. Vance felt rather than saw him coming, and the fifth and last chamber of the revolver was discharged with the muzzle almost against the priest's body. The latter dropped like an ox and lay motionless.

By this time the din and the smoke and the smell of gunpowder, mingled with groans from

one of the fallen men, had contributed to a
scene nothing short of infernal. Vance half
expected to find himself deserted by his companions and he felt that, in such event, he
could hardly blame them. It had been his
intention to warn Lirrhi of the nature of his
weapons as soon as he should be sufficiently
sure of his faith to be positive that no occasion
could arise when he might find it necessary to
launch their unknown terrors against a false
ally; but this certainty had not come until
very recently, and then events had occurred so
rapidly that the purpose had slipped his mind.

It was quickly evident, though, that these
island priests were made of a sterner stuff than
most savages, for, whatever might have been
the effect produced upon Lirrhi and Nhar by
the first shot, the last had scarcely been fired
and its victim down, before Vance felt someone
push by him from behind and glide forward
into the cloud of smoke that filled the chamber.

He knew that it must be Nhar, and his
knowledge was immediately confirmed, for an
instant later Lirrhi was beside him and answered his look of inquiry with:

" He has gone to find and kill the two who were sleeping—ah ! "

The sound of a short struggle came from the middle of the room, and then of a heavy body falling against and upsetting the table. The commotion disturbed the smoke which circled around in strata and lifted somewhat. Then they saw that one of the sleeping men must have staggered to his feet and, falling foul of Nhar, had been stabbed to death before he could realise what had happened.

The other could be dimly seen trying vainly to raise himself from his pallet but apparently overcome with wine or some narcotic. Nhar, who hitherto had been unable to quite get his bearings in the smoke, saw him at the same instant and sprang toward him with sword dripping blood, but scarcely had he reached the side of this last enemy when a sudden uproar arose in the opposite passage, and five more priests rushed out into the room choking with its atmosphere of burnt gunpowder and littered with the bodies of their dead and dying companions.

Their mantles had been thrown aside, their

swords were in their hands, and their shaven crowns shone oddly in the weird light. They paused a moment, as if to grasp the situation, clustered together at the entrance, and in that moment two things happened. Vance's second revolver had spoken and one of their number dropped, while Nhar, leaning over the pros- trate figure on the pallet, had drawn his weapon quickly across the fellow's throat.

The courage of these men seemed to the American something phenomenal. Unterrified by the mysterious agency that had stricken down their comrades and was now striking at them, unmindful even of death within the sacred precincts, they had no sooner realised half blindly what had happened and noted Nhar's act than, with one accord, they rushed furiously toward him.

What followed was all in an instant. The boy turned to fly and had reached the entrance of the passage where his friends were concealed, when he tripped over the body of one of the men whom Vance had shot. Before he could regain his footing, his four pursuers were upon him and he was literally stabbed to pieces by the swords that, in the blind fury of their wielders, wounded even allies by their frantic blows and thrusts.

During this sudden flight and pursuit, Vance had not dared to fire for fear of hitting the fugitive, but as the latter fell both he and Lirrhi rushed forward from their hiding-place. The revolver poured its four remaining streaks of flame across the room as they advanced, but, what with the hurried aim and the smoke that settled after the first shot, only one more of the priests fell. Another had his arm broken, but of the effect of these shots the assailants knew nothing when they plunged headlong into the clump of men who were still busy driving their weapons into the prostrate form of Nhar.

Then followed a confused *mêlée* in which blows and thrusts were given blindly and received almost without being felt. The three priests were fortunately the greater sufferers by reason of this blindness. Utterly ignorant of the number of their assailants and naturally despairing of escape, they lunged about in all directions with the frenzy of men bereft of their senses and swayed only by the animal instinct of fight.

Vance knew that he had run his sword through one man by the resistance to the thrust, and he knew the man had fallen by the weight upon its point as he drew the weapon back.   Lirrhi had, perhaps fortunately for himself, come full against one of his enemies without seeing him in the smoke, and, still more fortunately, it happened to be the one whose arm had been broken. The man had dropped his sword from his right hand and was groping on the floor for it with his left, when his assailant literally fell over him. He received another slight wound from Lirrhi's sword and then the two went down together, Lirrhi striving to shorten his blade for a new thrust, the other grasping at his enemy's throat with his sound hand and trying to choke him into insensibility.

Scarcely had Vance freed his weapon from the fellow before him when he heard a movement behind and, at the same moment, felt himself pierced just back of his shoulder but too high to do much harm. As he swung quickly around, his would-be slayer's sword caught sideways against shoulder-blade or clavicle and was wrenched from the hand that held it, while Vance, wheeling, struck with all his strength a long, sweeping blow in the direction of his adversary. It reached the priest's neck and clove downward almost to his chest. He, too, was harmless.

The Lieutenant, heedless of his wound, from which the weapon that inflicted it was still hanging, turned to look for his companion. As the smoke again began to lift, he made him out still struggling with his wounded enemy.

The latter was a powerful fellow, and, despite his injuries, had at last succeeded in getting uppermost. He was now endeavouring to wrench Lirrhi's sword from his fast relaxing grasp. Vance sprang toward them, and, grasping the man by the throat, hurled him aside, fetching a cut at his head as he fell which laid open the skull. Lirrhi struggled to his feet.

It was several moments before they were able to see clearly the shambles in which they stood, but, as soon as the prostrate forms that lay strewn around them became distinguishable, Lirrhi proceeded to examine them one by one, turning them upon their backs and peering into their faces distorted with the fury of combat and the death-agony. As he did so, one man opened his eyes and looked fixedly at him, and Vance, despite all the excitement and exhaustion, felt a new thrill of horror to see his companion deliberately draw his sword across the fellow's throat. Another, who groaned slightly, was treated in the same way, while the American leaned against the wall, too feeble to protest. This terrible inspection finished, Lirrhi rose and counted the bodies carefully.

"Ten," he said, and his brow contracted for a moment. "No, eleven," he added, after a pause. "I forgot the man you killed in the gallery. Well, there is one more."

CHAPTER XIX

THE HEART OF TAO

THERE was something in this announcement that seemed to save Vance from
sinking in his tracks. The strain and physical
exhaustion of the fight, superimposed upon
nerves weakened by the deep anxiety of the
last week, the knowledge that within a few
minutes he had, with his own hand, killed
nine men, not to mention the loss of blood
and the pain of his wound which, now that the
fighting was over, began to assert itself sharply,
all combined to overwhelm him. Nothing but
a consciousness that the work was still un-
finished could have revived his fainting energies, but this consciousness proved most
effective. He understood fully now just what
the escape of a single man meant; that it
meant the certainty of their being overpowered

in the bowels of the earth, without a chance
of escape, much less of success in their under-
taking, whatever that might be. Both he
and Lirrhi were more or less disabled, Nhar
was dead, while, as he mechanically reloaded
his revolvers, he could not but feel that the
moral effect of these weapons upon his adversaries had been practically worthless. They
were good for half a dozen more lives, and
that was about all.

The endurance of his companion, despite his
injury and the rough handling he had received,
was a source of astonishment to Vance only
less than was the desperate courage of their
enemies. Lirrhi seemed to have added
nothing to his physical hurt in the struggle
in which he had engaged, while his eyes and
movements told of an undiminished store of
nervous energy. He now busied himself in
stanching the blood that still flowed from the
Lieutenant's shoulder and in binding up the
wound with strips of a dead priest's gown.
This done, he seized a new torch from a niche
in the wall and proceeded to enter the opposite passage. Vance followed, having first

taken the precaution to reinforce his strength with a deep draught of wine, some of which still remained in one of the overturned flasks.

The gallery in which they now found themselves was similar to that from which they had entered the chamber of death, but its descent was far more precipitous. The air, too, seemed much denser and was charged with gaseous exhalations very sulphurous and stifling,— a bad exchange for even the gunpowder-impregnated atmosphere they were leaving behind. If there was a terrestrial entrance to the infernal regions, Vance felt that this path would be a much more realistic candidate for its honours than any of those described in verse or fiction from the *Æneid* to *Vathek*. Then he found himself smiling at the frivolity of his thoughts and wondering again at the proneness of the typical American, and more especially the American of the Middle States, to treat with an external flippancy emergencies which were really calling forth and absorbing his highest interest and energies. He had even begun to reason as to whether it might not be the result of some such overdraught on the nervous power

as produces hysterics in women.   Certainly it
was not an affectation, however it might have
the appearance of being such.

He was aroused from these irrelevant musings, which had served the purpose of resting
him somewhat, by a sudden and sharp declivity in the path.   For about two hundred feet
they were obliged to descend very carefully.
Then they came out upon a level floor of rock,
circular in shape,—a sort of smaller chamber,
but without the high, vaulted roof which had
made the former one noticeable.   This room
was no higher than the narrow passage that
led into it.   Its sides, too, were jagged and
uneven, with corners of rock jutting here and
there as if it had been, for some reason, more
hastily hewn out than the rest of the subterranean system.

The most remarkable feature of the place
was, however, one that seemed to mark it as
the termination of their path, for, on the
farther side from the passage by which they
had entered, Vance made out, instead of a
new gallery or even a barrier of rock, a huge
black pit which extended along the full width

of the chamber and prevented all further advance. When Lirrhi approached his torch close to the edge, the bottom of the abyss was visible not much more than twenty feet below the platform where they stood, but the descent was sheer and precipitous. The length and breadth of the chasm were not to be measured, for, though the gloom was illumined far around by the rays of the torch, there were yet blacker depths beyond.

He had only time to remark further and with some wonder that, from what he could see of the bottom and of the precipice that descended to it, the lava-rock that formed both was of a much later formation than any through which they had come, when Lirrhi grasped his arm and pointed to four bars of a metal that resembled bronze. These were affixed like levers close to the edge of the descent and near one side of the chamber. Three stood upright from the floor and were of moderate length, but the fourth, which projected horizontally from the wall a little back of the others, was much longer and heavier, as though intended to exert a much greater power. Vance saw, too, that there seemed to have been some appliance for moving them which could be worked from a distance.   There was a broad perforated flange in the end of each, as if to receive certain heavy hooks which he now noticed fastened to the ends of four ropes of woven metal which ran through holes in the wall behind him and were coiled neatly on the floor beneath.

He turned toward Lirrhi with an inquiring glace and was astonished to observe that his companion seemed to be labouring under some strong agitation.   His whole frame was trembling violently and his dark face had become almost ashen in hue.   All this and much more might have been looked for in any ordinary man, but Vance had, with good reason, come to regard the priest as altogether removed from most of the common emotions of humanity. The only time when he had appeared to show any feeling whatever was when expressing gratitude for his rescue from the ravine on the mountain, and the American felt instinctively that the present loss of self-control indicated some serious impending peril of which he himself was ignorant.   He was by this time, however, fully renerved to go through whatever might lie before him, and waited calmly for the next instructions.

Meanwhile the eyes of Lirrhi roved furtively around the chamber. A look of absolute terror was evident in their dusky depths, but, after a few moments of hesitation, he seemed to recover something of his composure, and, again pointing to the levers, said, in a low voice:

" Thrust them forward, one by one, — the small ones first. It is the last effort and the most perilous. May your god give you strength to move the great one."

Without delay Vance set himself to accomplish the task imposed. The three small levers yielded with very little effort and were, one by one, turned down level with the floor.

" Now the other! Quick! quick! " cried Lirrhi. " The gases are freed. The torrent must be turned under the sea."

Without realising in the least the meaning of his companion's words, Vance threw his weight against the great bronze bar. He could not perceive that it moved even a hair's breadth. Lirrhi became almost frantic as he saw that the first effort was a failure.

" Again! again!" he shrieked. " All your strength! It is for three men, but you *must* move it. One hundred pulse-beats, and the death-vapours will be here and we shall die."

Again Vance bent himself to the task with all the nervous force that the combined passions of love and fear could lend. Surely the bar seemed to stir slightly, and Lirrhi, who up to this point had been only holding the torch and urging his companion on, now rushed forward and laid his hand on the metal, as if to add his strength to the effort. Then suddenly he sprang back with a cry of warning.

Vance caught the words " The twelfth priest!" and, turning his head, he saw bounding toward him this sole survivor of the guardians of the mountain. The man's cloak had been thrown aside and, with gleaming eyes, drawn blade, and red tunic girded up, he seemed to the intruder's startled gaze like the demon presiding over the pit to which they had so rashly penetrated. He had doubtless been hiding all the time behind some projection of the uneven walls.

Everything passed like a flash. When the eyes of the American first saw the peril, his enemy was already within four or five feet. Another spring would bring him upon him and he could feel the sharp blade piercing his back and drawn across his throat. Instinctively he threw himself to one side, and so quickly that the body of the other was carried by its impetus full against the lever with so much force as to be completely doubled up across it.

Almost at the same moment, Vance, recovering his feet, sprang upon the fellow's back and, having no time to draw sword or pistol, sought only by grasping the long bar with both hands to hold his assailant helpless over it until Lirrhi could return and cut his throat in the most effective manner. The result was one upon which he had not calculated. The momentum of the two bodies coming almost at the same moment upon the lever, seemed to supply the power which had been lacking to one alone. Creaking, it swung slowly around.

The effect was startling beyond anything that had yet happened. The whole mountain shuddered and rocked as if under the influence of some tremendous force, while a dull, heavy roar like the rush and fall of a cataract of molten lead came rumbling to Vance's ears, increasing every instant in volume and nearness.

He half turned his head to see why Lirrhi was delaying so long to come to his rescue and release him from his awkward position. To his amazement and dismay, he saw that his companion, usually so cool and courageous, had turned and, as if possessed by unreasoning terror, was scrambling wildly up the steep passage.

Left to his own resources and impressed with a sense of impending peril, though without realising its nature, the American loosed his grasp upon the bar, and, raising the half-limp form of his prisoner in his arms, he swung him round and, with a violent effort, hurled him over into the abyss. One piercing shriek of indescribable fear and horror rang in his ears high above the swelling din that surrounded him, and then, with every sense gone except the instinct of self-preservation, he turned and darted up the ascent in pursuit of the fleeing Lirrhi.

The latter had already disappeared, but the light of the torch which he still carried shone dimly along the gallery and indicated that he could not be far in advance.

Stumbling, recovering himself again, tearing his garments and even his flesh against projecting points of rock, Vance clambered and ran onward. It seemed ages before he could overtake the other. At last, as he reached the level, he caught sight of the priest struggling on ahead and staggering from side to side like a drunken man. A strong, suffocating odour began to permeate the dense air while the roaring behind increased every second.

Vance now gained rapidly, but, at the moment when only a stride separated the two, Lirrhi stopped short, swayed in his tracks and then sank slowly down, while his companion sprang forward just in time to grasp the torch and save it from extinguishment. The priest turned upon him an eye glazed with terror, and gasped faintly:

" Quick—the way we came, and out! No one can breathe it and live."

Hardly knowing what he did, the American stooped down and, picking up in his arms the now senseless form, resumed his flight. Everything was whirling in his brain. His hand still grasped the torch but his eyes were blind to its light. At one time he became vaguely conscious that he was crossing the first chamber, where the combat had taken pace. Twice he stumbled over dead men and once almost came to the ground with his burden. Ghostly shrieks mingled with triumphant laughter assailed him and he imagined that the hands of the corpses reached up and grasped his tunic and tried to drag him down among them until he wrenched himself loose and pursued his way.

At another moment he found himself gravely doubting whether he, too, was not really dead and endeavouring to escape from some hell into which he had fallen, while, to add to his confusion, the torch, either by brushing against the wall or by being burned out, was suddenly extinguished.

How the remainder of the path was covered he never knew; but at last a narrow streak of light became visible, — light that in the outer world doubtless would have been called " darkness," but which seemed brilliantly luminous amid the dense gloom of this subterranean gallery. For a moment his senses rallied. He was at the great revolving rock that had closed the entrance to the passage, and which they fortunately had not swung quite shut. Still the fugitive knew nothing of how to move the mass from the inside and could only hurl himself blindly against it.

The delicacy with which the balance had been adjusted stood him in good stead, for the rock, seeming to take pity upon his exhaustion, yielded slowly, and Vance, still holding the inanimate form of Lirrhi in what was almost his own death-grasp, fell rather than passed through the widening aperture. Then he dropped like a log, and even instinct left him.

CHAPTER XX

MARSHALLED FOES

TO experience all the feelings of a violent death and yet to return to life is a knowledge not lacking to humanity and least of all to the soldier; but the scenes of blood and almost supernatural terror through which Vance had passed were of a nature far beyond the lines of even extraordinary suffering, and the collapse that followed them was utter and complete.

The first indication of returning consciousness that came to him was a sense of dull pain throbbing, throbbing in his shoulder and shooting thence, from time to time, through all the nerves of his body. As he drifted slowly back from the dark world of nothingness, the pain increased until his lips were forced apart in a groan.

The effort seemed to arouse him still more. He opened his eyes, but a dazzling light made him close them again. He knew that his head rested on someone's knees. The bright glare burned through his closed lids. Gradually, as he became accustomed to it, it seemed to grow more dim, and at last he again ventured to look up. This attempt was attended with better success. He was now able to bear what he knew could only be the daylight, and that, too, filtered through the network of vines that covered the outer passage. Lirrhi's dark face and deep eyes, again inscrutable and expressionless, were above him, though it was hard to realise that the features were those he had seen only a short time since contorted and blanched by succeeding waves of fury and terror. Perhaps they both were really dead, after all, he thought, and it was the priest's spirit that had resumed its calm.

The neck of a flask thrust between his teeth served, however, to dispel any illusion that clung to his gathering reason, and the draught soon restored him to the full knowledge that he was alive and suffering, as well as served to recall the memory of what had occurred and, above all, of Zelkah. Strength, too, came with that thought, such as no spirits could infuse.

" What has happened ? Did we succeed ? Is she safe ? " he asked.

" There is more to be done," said Lirrhi slowly.

Vance was on his feet in a moment. The nerves that had given out when the end seemed to have been attained resumed at once their stimulating power.

" Very well. I am ready," he said shortly.

Lirrhi remained seated and viewed him curiously for a moment. An expression as closely akin to astonishment as the priest's face admitted of was apparent on his features, and Vance, following his companion's eyes, glanced down at himself.

It was then that he first realised to the full what had taken place. His tunic, the only garment he still retained, hung in tatters about him and its rags were thick with earth-stains and caked with the blood of himself and his enemies. His priest's sword had been lost from his belt, but his own and his pistols were still safe. An impulse to laugh heartily at his condition and at that of Lirrhi, who was but little better off, was checked by a sharper twinge from the wounded shoulder,—a twinge that seemed to traverse his frame, stopping now and again to exchange compliments with the numerous minor cuts and bruises it encountered on its route.

"Can you travel and fight more?" his companion asked at last.

"You see I can stand," replied Vance, "and I think I can draw a trigger."

He glanced toward his revolvers, and Lirrhi, catching the inference, said:

"You fight with the thunder and lightning. They are good weapons. Tao has not taught his chosen how to govern them."

An expression of cynical contempt shaded the speaker's face. Vance interpreted it to indicate what in civilisation would be termed an advanced condition of scepticism on the priest's part. Certainly he could hardly believe in a god against whom he consented to fight and whose apparent manifestations were

so evidently the result of priestly chicanery.
Still, it was evident that he was enough of a
believer in something to dread dying upon
the mountain and to feel the strongest gratitude for being saved from that fate.   Vance
had not yet ceased to wonder at the courage
of all these men when brought face to face
with so mysterious an agency of destruction as
gunpowder; though possibly he might have
better comprehended Lirrhi's other attributes
had he reflected how inconsistently scepticism
and superstition are sometimes mingled in in-
dividuals of more enlightened races.

" Come," said Vance, finally, as he saw the
other lapsing into deep thought, " you can
count upon me to last as long as there is work
to be done, but all the same it would be just
as well to finish it as soon as possible.   How
about your side ? " he added, after a pause,
during which Lirrhi said nothing.   " Has it
received further hurt ?   Can you still count
upon yourself ? "   The prospect of again
carrying his companion rather shook his new
confidence in his strength, and yet even in that
contingency there would be nothing to do

17

but to pursue his task until it or he was finished. He was quickly reassured on this point,
however, for Lirrhi sprang to his feet with an
agility which he himself could not have imitated.

" I think the bone has knit better in the
last few hours," said the priest. " The bandages are well put on and they are still in place.
Do not fear but that I shall be strong as long
as is necessary; we islanders are all trained to
endure; but let me look at your wound first."

With skilful fingers, and rapidly, he made
an examination.

" It is not so very bad," he said. " It will
not disable you if you do not mind the pain."

" That is nothing," replied Vance, with a
grimace, as Lirrhi proceeded to work the
shoulder-joint.

" You must be careful not to let it stiffen
yet," he added. " No bone is hurt and no
great muscle divided. The blood, too, has
ceased to flow. What did you do with the
last priest ? "

" I threw him into the chasm," said Vance.
Lirrhi shuddered.

" Ah ! " he continued, after a pause. " He

has journeyed to the ocean, then, in a coffin of lava.   Let us go on.''

They started down the ravine and, whether the effort of motion or the renewal of nerve-force was responsible, Vance felt himself grow stronger with each step.   He took occasion, too, to follow the good advice he had received as to moving the hurt shoulder, which he did, gritting his teeth together, and gently at first so as not to reopen the wound.   He soon found that Lirrhi had been right as to the nature of the injury, and by the time he had reached the entrance his left arm seemed almost as useful as his right.   The soreness had abated, and only a slight exercise of will-power was necessary to render his whole body serviceable, if not sound.

Several times on the way he had made an effort to question his companion and to obtain some definite notion of what they had accomplished, how it had been done, and in what way it affected their ultimate aim.   He was conscious of, and still irritated somewhat by the fact that he had been used all along as a mere automaton, and had done nothing but obey orders blindly,— kill when told to, and defend himself when attacked. Of course he was now fully assured of the priest's good faith, but he felt that his own efforts might have been and would still be much more effi-cient had he more than the vaguest idea of what might be their aim.

Lirrhi, however, had relapsed, if the term could be used of him, into his non-committal mood. In fact, he did not even seem to hear the questions addressed to him. Only when they had crawled again through the hole by which they had entered the ravine and stepped out several paces into the open ground, he laid his hand upon Vance's arm and pointed to the crater above them. Just a slender thread of vapour wound its way upward from the summit, to be lost in the blue vault above without obscuring its deep azure by so much as the thinnest film. The eruption had ceased entirely.

Vance turned inquiringly toward the priest.

" That is our work thus far," said Lirrhi.

Without another word, he turned again and led the way down the descent.

Vance asked no further questions. He had learned that these were useless so far as procuring or even hastening information from his companion was concerned; and so they walked on in silence, though the active mind of the American was beginning, unaided, to conceive the almost inconceivable truth.

Upon reaching the level ground once more, the journey became easier. They again struck the broad, paved road leading to the city, and soon the glint of sunlight on its white walls gladdened their eyes. Unconsciously they walked faster, until at last they passed under the shadow of the gate through which they had set out on the evening before.

Vance noticed carelessly that the streets along which they were hurrying were almost deserted, and, from the curious glances which a few women whom they met bestowed upon his certainly startling appearance, he congratulated himself very heartily that most of the inhabitants were otherwise employed. Soon a low, humming sound, as of many voices, came to their ears. The square was now but a short distance ahead. Evidently it was there that the people were assembled, and in greater numbers than ever.

Another corner was turned, and then the outskirts of the crowd appeared, extending far down the street. It seemed impossible to penetrate farther. Lirrhi spoke to a man who stood with his back to them, trying illogically enough to look over the heads of those in front to where a corner of wall blotted out even more effectively whatever might be going on beyond.

" Will you tell me, friend, the cause of this commotion ? "

The Karanian turned and surveyed them from head to foot in open-mouthed astonishment. At first glance he took them both to be priests and in most desperate plight. Then his eyes fastened upon certain spots where blood or water had removed the dark stain from Vance's face and body or where it had been scraped off in the contact with man and rock.

" The stranger! " he ejaculated.

" But what are the people gathered for ? " asked Lirrhi again.

The man looked blankly at him.

" I do not know," he said. " I saw others running and I followed."

" Tao is appeased," explained a bystander who had been attracted by the conversation, " and Merrak and Aroo have summoned the people to give thanks. The maid must have died quickly."

" Nonsense! " cried another. " A man who ran by me said that Aroo had slain the Soveet."

The crowd was becoming more excited, and, as whispers passed from mouth to mouth, the angry feeling against the American as the cause of their trouble began to take form again, and threatening eyes were bent upon him from many sides. At the same moment a louder uproar came from the square in front.

" Listen! " cried Lirrhi earnestly, addressing those nearest him. " I am a priest. This man is protected by Tao until Tao shall order him slain. Has not Aroo proclaimed as much ? I have been ordered, even now, to bring him at once to where the Soveet and high-priest deliberate as to his fate. You see with what trouble I have secured him. Make way for Tao's captive! Make way!"

With an assumption of authority, he started to push through the crowd, whispering hurriedly in Vance's ear:

" It is necessary for us to reach the Soveet at once."

Those around gave way sullenly at these words, and their glances toward the supposed prisoner became more hostile but less threatening. Farther on, however, the press grew denser, and new explanations had to be made at every step. Lirrhi was almost beginning to despair.

Then it was that a very timely manifestation of the speed with which a rumour makes its way through a crowd came to his rescue. A great murmur of voices in mingled tones of command and expostulation rose suddenly from the midst of the square and rolled nearer and nearer. Soon they could make out by the increasing pressure that some commotion was going on ahead. The mass of human beings surged hither and thither, while a cry of

" Make way for the Soveet's men! " could be distinguished now above the din.

It was evident that a party clothed with authority was forcing a passage through the throng and advancing slowly toward where the priest and Vance had almost ceased their efforts to make further headway.   The two now awaited whatever was to develop.

It came quickly.   First there was a wilder jostling and confusion; the struggle of those in front to get out of the way seemed to extend its influence all through the multitude, as a wave rolls over the ocean.   At last the head of a company of nobles came in view, and, what with hoarse commands, sturdy press- ure, and an occasional prick with their sharp swords, it soon worked its way to the place where Lirrhi and his companion stood.

The officer in command eyed the adventur- ers with a look of indecision.   At last he said:

" Are you Lirrhi, the priest of Tao ? "

Lirrhi bowed.

" And this man ?   Is he the stranger from the sea ? " continued the officer, indicating Vance, but with even more hesitation.

" You have said the truth," replied Lirrhi;
" and he demands to be taken at once before
the Soveet on a matter of high importance
that will admit of no delays."

A sinister smile curled the Karanian's
bearded lips.

" I was sent to bring him," he said shortly.
" Rumour ran that he was among the people.
Let him pray his god that whatever other demands he may have shall be granted as readily
as this one."

He turned and addressed a few words to his
followers, who proceeded at once to clear a
space and to get Lirrhi and Vance in their
midst. Then they began their journey back
through the crowd, like a ship in the waves of
a sea that close in upon her wake as fast as her
prow dashes the water aside.

Meanwhile that part of the square directly
in front of the Soveet's house and from which
most of the noise had proceeded, became comparatively silent. It seemed as though the
contending elements had subsided until the
newcomers should appear upon the scene.

As they drew nearer, Vance saw that the

terrace above the long steps was thronged back to the very palace gates with rank upon rank of the nobles, and several paces in advance of these he distinguished Merrak himself, seated upon a low throne. The building, too, appeared to be garrisoned, while the huge black temple near it frowned portentously. At last the party broke through the inner circle of the crowd and came out into an open space at the foot of the steps, which a large force of guards was with great difficulty keeping clear.

Aroo, surrounded by a score of his followers, stood in this area, facing the Soveet, who, supported as he was by armed men of his own race, looked calmly down at his rival. Close by the former was an officer who held in his hand a tablet such as Vance had seen Lirrhi affix to the post near the palace before setting out for the mountain.

As soon as they had come to a halt, the American shot a quick glance around the crowd, to draw, if possible, from the nearest faces an intimation of its temper and of the nature of the matters impending. He saw with some misgivings that the front ranks were composed entirely of priests, among whom the sentiments of anger and solicitude seemed to alternate. It was quite evident that they either had been or feared they were about to be attacked, if not in their persons, at least in their power and privileges.

The time for inspection was short. A look of satisfaction flashed across the Soveet's face when he saw that his men had secured the persons sent for. Then, as his eyes rested for a moment upon Vance, he frowned heavily. At the same moment Aroo turned, but whether his forbidding features expressed fear, hate, triumph, or all combined was not easy to tell. Whatever the expression was, it passed as quickly as it came, and with calm brow he once more confronted the Soveet.

The latter now made a signal to the officer who held the tablet and the man stepped forward and glanced inquiringly at his Prince. Merrak spoke:

" In the presence now of accuser and accused, and before me and my people, let the charge be read."

CHAPTER XXI

THE MASSACRE

THE words of the Soveet could not have penetrated far, but the action of his secretary, for such he seemed to be, carried a fuller significance. A deep silence fell over the crowded square, as the latter proceeded to read in a loud, ringing voice:

" I denounce and defy the false god, Tao, and Aroo, his priest, and all that obey him to make blood flow. Ere morning comes Tao shall bow to my power and return to his bonds while the maid is yet alive. Punish his followers who have deceived the people and conspired against thy race. So saith the stranger."

No outburst of anger followed this audacious charge; but to an experienced man the silence that continued to prevail was more threatening than the wildest uproar. It was probable that

the vast multitude looked to see some vengeance so terrible fall upon the blasphemer, that
their indignation against his act was well-nigh
lost in what was almost pity for his impending
fate.   Then, too, some, doubtless, were filled
with consternation lest Tao, in his blind wrath,
should confound the innocent with the guilty
in one awful holocaust of fire and death.

Second after second passed in weird silence.
The sky was still bright and clear, and the
thread of vapour that had pencilled from Tao's
mouth was now so faint as to be almost indis-
cernible.   Perhaps, after all, the god would
leave his vindication in the hands of his children, for at that moment Aroo's voice rose
strident and menacing:

" In the name of Tao, I demand that the
sacrilegious stranger be given up to be thrust
into the mouth of the god whom he has blas-
phemed! "

Again there was silence.   To the people it
must have seemed that the high-priest was lax
in his duty, to ask so mild a sentence.   The
affair would end in an anticlimax after all.

As for Vance, he was rather disposed to

think that his last hour had come. He began
to consider seriously whether he should not at
once empty all the chambers of one revolver
into Aroo's body and thus insure the punishment of the arch-villain, rather than attempt a
personal defence which must be hopeless. The
Soveet finally broke the silence.

" Let the stranger speak for himself," he
said.

Aroo sprang forward. His composure was
gone, and his dark face flamed with passion.
Raising his hand, he cried out:

" You will hear him ? You will permit him
to re-utter the blasphemies you have already
listened to ? Take warning! Tao has for-
borne long, but there will be an end of forbearance."

The Soveet seemed to vacillate. His eye
wandered from the high-priest to Vance and
then over the sea of faces that, still silent and
intent, waited anxiously to see and hear the
end.

" Has not the stranger fulfilled his promise,
O Soveet ? Go now and fetch home the maid."

These words, spoken by a voice which had

till then been unheard, came like an electric shock to the tense-drawn nerves of all. The speaker was Lirrhi, who now advanced toward the throne and stood with arms folded across his chest and eyes fixed upon the Soveet's face, until it seemed to colour slowly under the set gaze.

Among the crowd, both of nobles upon and above the steps, and of priests and people below in the square, there was not one but had noted the fact; only their confused minds had not grasped its full import. Instinctively every man turned his head in the direction of the mountain, and a confused murmur, gathering slowly in volume, rose, as if to relieve the situation. Still, though the words of Lirrhi, uttered at such a time and enforced by such ocular evidence, produced of necessity a deep impression, the revulsion of feeling seemed by no means general. The powers of superstition were not to be so easily overthrown, and the priests in particular pressed closer upon the open space and, with threatening faces and gestures, began slowly to force the guards back toward the steps.

Upon Aroo himself, however, the effect of Lirrhi's words was most startling. For a moment he gazed in dumb astonishment at this assault from a presumably friendly quarter. Then, as his cunning reasserted itself, and he realised the inevitable influence of such a speech, a glimmer of the truth as to what must have happened, and through what agency, seemed to cross his mind. Instantly every vestige of calm and self-control left him. Hatred and fear made his face seem almost demoniacal. His sword flashed from his belt, and, screaming the single word " Traitor! " he sprang, like a cat, upon the man who had deserted his caste.

Lirrhi and those around him stood as if paralysed by the sudden onslaught. Then came the blinding flash and ring of a pistol-shot. A cloud hung over the open space. Shrieks and groans resounded through the square, and many covered their faces. Tao had at last smitten the impious stranger, and they waited till he should be pleased to claim such other victims as might appease his wrath. Above all were evident the stolid resignation

18

and fatalistic calm of the islanders.   No one in the square dreamed of escaping.   Had such an impulse gained sway, thousands would have been crushed to death; but the situation was to their minds simply this: their god was angry; he would slay whom he willed, and they could not escape him; therefore they abided his pleasure.

In a moment more the breeze had swept the smoke away, and those who ventured to look saw a spectacle to them incomprehensible. Lirrhi stood there unharmed.   The impious foreigner whom they themselves had seen enveloped in the fire hurled down to destroy him stood by the priest's side with a small piece of metal, still smoking faintly, in his hand; while, writhing upon the ground directly at their feet, was the all-powerful Aroo, the favourite son of Tao.

The mass of nobles upon the steps had, in a moment of terror, given evidence of their different lineage from the people.   Many of them had sought to escape and much confusion prevailed in their ranks.   Finally, however, those who were unwilling to desert their

monarch and those who were able to realise the
fatality which a panic would induce, regained
the ascendancy; especially when it was observed that the destroyer had stayed his hand.

Aroo was struggling to rise. He had been
shot through the body, and his face was
contorted with agony through which still
shone hatred and unconquerable will. Once
he gained his knees, only to sink back. Vance
watched him with set eyes. Suddenly, by a
frightful effort, the high-priest struggled to his
feet, swaying to and fro for an instant. A
steely glitter was in his eye, and he lowered
his head like a wounded bull about to charge.
Lirrhi's gaze was fixed upon Vance with all
the intensity of a hypnotiser's, and the latter,
scarcely conscious of what he was doing, raised
the pistol again, placed it almost against his
enemy's breast, and fired. Aroo dropped in a
heap and, after one or two convulsive shud-
ders, lay still. Lirrhi's pent-up feelings burst
forth in a deep sigh, while Vance looked
vacantly around him like a man just awakened
from slumber. Then his eyes fell upon the
corpse and wandered to the smoking pistol.

His face grew firm and determined, and he turned defiantly toward the crowd.

The second shot, while fully justified by the set intent and probable ability of Aroo to effect harm, the futility of any attempt to evade him in the small space, and the helplessness or unwillingness of those around to restrain the wounded man's fury, was nevertheless, in one sense, unfortunate. It made clearly apparent Vance's agency in what most of the people had before believed to be the stroke of some mysterious power. At once the priests began to throng tumultuously forward, brandishing their swords and forcing the guards before them by the tremendous pressure of the mass behind.

Vance and Lirrhi backed slowly toward the steps and, ascending, pushed their way into the front rank of the nobles, who stood uncertain what to do and waiting for some word from the Soveet, who seemed to be entirely stunned by what had taken place.

At length, when the priest-led mob had already mounted the first step and the guards were being crowded back upon the main body

of their fellows, Lirrhi's voice rose again above
the uproar that had been rapidly gaining
strength and volume. Having worked his way
to where the Soveet sat with head sunk upon
his breast, he cried out:

" Let the people pause and listen."

For a moment the noise and confusion
subsided.

" Have I permission to speak ? " he continued, addressing Merrak.

The latter bowed his head and said, in a low
voice:

" Yes, yes; speak to them."

" To them and to you," shouted Lirrhi, at
the same time turning and facing the square,
" that all may know how the stranger has overthrown the impostors. He saved me from
death, and therefore have I aided him against
a murderer and disclosed all the evil of which
I had learned the secret. Let those who believe that it was Tao's wrath which caused the
mountain to flame and thunder know now that
it was only the wrath of Aroo and those who
preceded him——"

A terrible uproar arose among the priests at

these words.   Some tried to drown the accusing voice with wild cries; others endeavoured to break through the guard, which, now supported by the throng upon the steps, could be forced no farther and presented a solidly packed front.   Then, too, the people in the square had been listening with a dazed look upon their faces.   They no longer supplied the weight of their dense mass to back up the forward movement of the priests.   Had they done so, it must have been irresistible, and the square would soon have been piled high with the bodies of men suffocated or crushed to death.

" It was Aroo that longed for the death of the Soveet's daughter," continued Lirrhi, raising his voice above the noises that contended against it; " Aroo and those favourite sons of Tao who went before him and who, to humble and keep down the power of the men from the sea, devised the sacrifice and bored their galleries into Tao's bosom and wrought cunning mechanisms by which the explosive gases might be restrained and let loose at will and the fire-streams turned under the ocean or hurled high in air and rolled down upon the country."

For a moment the square had been almost silent, as if the outburst of sound was pausing to gather headway that it might overwhelm these terrible revelations, but meanwhile a glimmer of the import of what he had heard seemed to pierce the Soveet's brain, and, with it, a sudden consciousness of its truth. To many of those around him came a similar conviction, as is often the case in a crowd that listens, open - mouthed, until in an instant a thought darts through its utmost confines, reaching by some subtle man-to-man influence even those who have not heard the words that first called it into being.

As if inspired with all the quick resolve and activity of youth, the Prince who had been so feeble and vacillating before the dread of an unseen power sprang from his seat and cried out:

" Let every son of Tao be secured!"

Some of the priests, farther-sighted or more timid than the rest, had taken advantage of the time during which these events had been occurring to work their way back into the crowd; but the great majority, confident in the strength of their prestige and never dreaming that matters would assume a really dangerous phase for them as a caste, had been violent and aggressive up to the very moment of the Soveet's command. Then, all at once, they realised their peril. In the square the nobles outnumbered them five to one, but the black temple was held by a strong garrison, and the mountain with its heights and honeycombed depths offered a refuge from which a long defence might be maintained.

The trouble was that between them and both mountain and temple was packed a dense mass of human beings which ordinarily would be unable to empty itself out of the square for an hour at least. There seemed to be but one chance.

Fortunately, or unfortunately, the islanders of the native race were, by ancient laws, forbidden to bear arms. Years since, during the constantly onward march of priestly encroachments, this right had been conceded to the

priesthood; and, as Vance learned later, at the
very time of the landing Aroo had almost
brought to a head certain schemes of his own
which would have resulted in the disarming of
the nobles, leaving his followers the only persons on the island capable of prompt attack or
defence. He had hardly reckoned upon ac-
complishing this final stroke without violence,
but for that he had about prepared himself
when the coming of the *Falcon* had compelled
him to postpone his *coup*.

Had the common people been armed, it
would perhaps have been a question as to
which side would have gained their assistance,
— whether racial kinship or sense of justice
would have prevailed. Probably, in view of
the facts that not one man in fifty had heard
or seen what had taken place, and that to most
of those who had heard, no clear comprehen-
sion of it all was possible, the priesthood could
have counted pretty confidently upon the support of an armed mob.

This fact their leaders knew; but then the
mob was *not* armed. It could be of little or no
assistance. They must escape from the trap in

which they were caught, and the only path was through the people.

By a system of sign-orders cunningly devised by Aroo as a part of the machinery to gain his ambitious ends, the whole body of priests was suddenly concentrated, faced about, and then hurled with terrific force upon the crowd.   All this passed before the nobles had formed in sufficient force to execute the Soveet's command,—by no means an easy one at best.

Under the impact of a mass welded together in such close order and presenting, as far as possible, a wedge-like front, the people were hurled aside, thrown down, and trampled under foot, or forced back, crushed and gasping.   Even the swords were used to prick into more active co-operation those who were slower to give way; for the priestly leaders doubtless reasoned that if the crowd could be made to trample and crush itself to death, they and their followers would escape with greater speed and less wear and tear.

For a few moments these tactics seemed likely to prevail.   The weight, solidity, and formation of the assailing ranks carried them at first far into the square, as a rifle-bullet would pierce a bank of loose sand. A panic, too, very naturally prevailed, and no man was in their path who did not endeavour vigorously to escape and make way for the human battering-ram that assailed him and his fellows.

But neither inclination, fear, nor force was sufficient to overcome for long the helpless resistance of a great body of men packed in a circumscribed space. There were those far in the rear to whom sufficient speed could not be communicated rapidly enough and whose movements, even when made, were almost as likely to impede as to expedite the opening of the way sought.

Soon the column of fugitives, like the same rifle-ball shot into the sand-bank, found itself brought to a stand. Then, furious at the opposition, involuntary though it was, and reckless of the fate of friends or foes, those in the front rank began to use their swords in earnest and were soon clambering onward over heaps of bleeding corpses.

The people had submitted with their usual stolidity to be crushed and trampled to death by their spiritual guides.   Doubtless even good will had had as much to do with their readiness to clear a way as had the violence with which that way had been demanded; but now, with weapons gleaming before their eyes and being plunged again and again into the bosoms of neighbours and friends, wrath and despair took the place of submission and terror.   They turned savagely upon their assailants; they clung to their raised arms; they wound themselves about their feet, and brought them down in that press to fall beneath which meant never to arise; they sought to choke them with their strong, nervous hands; they thrust their fingers into their eyes, tore their faces with their nails, and tried to bite them.   Many fell; but slaughter itself becomes exhausting in time, and then, the greater the piles of corpses, the more effort to climb over them.   The onward impetus of the column was at last checked, and at the same moment the nobles, regaining their presence of mind and urged on by the now impetuous Merrak, poured down from the terrace and fell furiously upon its rear.

Then followed a scene too bloody to admit of description. Making prisoners was no longer thought of. The sight and smell of slaughter had driven away any such mild intention, and, besides, there were years of political encroachment to be avenged, years of presumptuous insolence from inferiors which must be washed away in crimson waves.

The priests were now packed so closely by the pressure on all sides that it had become almost impossible for them to use their swords, much less for the rearmost ranks to face about against their enemies. It was a double massacre, rather than a battle. The priests slew the unarmed populace, the nobles slew the equally helpless priests.

To Vance, the weirdest feature of it all was the silence with which the terrible work was accomplished. A few shouts were uttered by the assailing nobles, but from these strangely stoical islanders not a shriek told of their sufferings. Even the groans of the wounded and dying were stifled so long as consciousness remained, and the most definite sound that he heard — a sound that grated in his ears long after that day — was the noise of the swords cutting and thrusting through flesh and bone.

CHAPTER XXII

THE HOUSE OF TAO

WHILE Vance's eyes were fastened in horror upon the awful work going on before them, he became suddenly conscious of some one calling his name as if from a great distance. Thus summoned to himself, he glanced around. The last of the nobles had already swept by the spot where he stood. He was alone, except for the corpse of Aroo, which lay almost at his feet, and for Lirrhi, who had sunk down upon the steps in a condition of utter collapse. It was the latter who had just spoken, but in a voice so weak as hardly to attract his companion's attention.

Stepping quickly to the side of the priest, he half raised him in his arms and peered anxiously into his face. It was very pale, but the eyes still shone. With an effort, he

brought his lips close to Vance's ear and whispered slowly but distinctly:

"Hurry! Do you not know? The house
of Tao! They will send messengers there."

Vance started as the meaning flashed upon
him. Some of the priests must doubtless have
escaped and such would naturally make their
way as quickly as possible to tell their tale to
those who guarded the Princess. He shuddered to think of the prompt and certain result
of their vengeance and fury.

Still, he could not bring himself to desert
his apparently dying friend, more especially as
the priestly garb alone would at such a time
be sure to expose the man wearing it to every
indignity at the hands of the triumphant
nobles. Lirrhi noticed the hesitation and
guessed its cause. A smile crossed his features, and with a new effort he said in a louder
voice:

"I tell you, you must hasten or she is lost.
I am well,—only exhausted. I shall live."

At that moment Vance saw a man in the
dress of a noble hurrying from the door of the
palace, and, as he came near, the Lieutenant

recognised the face of Esbal and called out to
him.   The grim mariner of the galley stopped
suddenly at the sound of his name, and approached the spot where Vance stood.   The
latter pointed to Lirrhi and said:

" Get the women from the palace to attend
to him, and guard his safety with your life.
It is the Soveet's order."

Then, without giving the other an opportunity to reply or question, and surmising that
he would not be likely to take the risk of dis-
obeying so simple a command, the American
turned away and, bounding down to where the
rearmost ranks of the nobles were pressing onward after their fellows, he shouted:

" Follow me!   To the Princess! "

A score of men halted and, turning, eyed
him curiously.   Then his meaning seemed to
flash through the minds of some of them, and
as he ran swiftly along the base of the terrace
a dozen armed followers gathered at his heels.
Casting one backward glance to where he had
left Lirrhi, he saw that Esbal had taken the
priest in his arms and was mounting the steps,
and then, his mind relieved of at least one of

its troubles, he plunged into a side street, followed closely by his band of volunteers.

Gradually the noise of combat grew fainter, until, by the time they had reached the gate, there was nothing to indicate that the people were busied otherwise than about their customary callings.

Vance at once struck the road that led through the plantations and villas toward the heights overshadowing the city. The clouds floated lazily across the sky; the birds flitted from spray to spray, and chirped and sang of everything except war and slaughter. Even such rustics as had not been unfortunate enough to go to town ceased from their work and looked in wonder at the company of armed men who, with tunics girt up, bent bodies, and set faces, ran silently by. One fellow alone seemed to grasp the situation.

" You will have to run fast to catch them," he cried. " They are both naked."

" Who ? " shouted Vance, as he passed.

" The thieves, to be sure," replied the other.

Evidently at least two priests were in advance and had thrown aside their garments

that they might move more swiftly, while the
peasant had surmised from Vance's torn and
bloody appearance that he had been set upon
by thieves, in pursuit of whom he was now
leading the agents of justice.

Since his first cry for help, no word had
passed between the American and his followers.
Once suggested, the situation was perfectly
apparent to all; and the receipt of this new
and most disquieting information only caused
them to draw their breath more deeply and increase their speed.   If the fleeing messengers
reached the house of Tao before them, there
would be little room to hope; but then, on the
other hand, the fellows could not know that
they were so closely tracked, and there was a
chance that they might not exert themselves
to the full.

And now the heights were gained, the cultivated ground was left behind and the pursuers
found themselves running in Indian file along
the narrow wood-path by which their leader
had first gained the mountain.   More than
half the distance from the city gate to their
destination must have been covered when a

.sudden turn brought them in view of the
quarry,—two priests, with all their clothing
and arms thrown aside, running about twenty
yards ahead.

Almost before the men had grasped the fact
that enemies were nearly upon them, Vance
drew a pistol and fired. The ball must have
gone wide, and one of the priests bounded forward with increased speed. The other, however, slackened his pace for a moment and cast
a frightened glance over his shoulder. The
action was fatal. Again the pistol cracked, and
this time with some effect for the fellow began
to limp as he ran. Then his legs seemed to
give way under him and he stumbled and fell.

Vance sprang over his prostrate victim and
dashed on in pursuit of the other; but the lust
of blood was upon him now in its full force,
and it was with a feeling of distinct satisfaction
that he understood, without even looking back,
that the first of his followers had halted long
enough to run his sword several times through
the body of the wounded man. His mind was
thoroughly awake, and his body seemed as
strong and active as if the preceding night had

been spent comfortably in bed instead of in
giving and receiving wounds and in deadly
combat with the most terrible forces of nature.
One thing now struck him forcibly, as, pistol
in hand, he watched eagerly for a glimpse of
the other messenger through the foliage. It
certainly would never do for his whole following to maintain their present speed and come
weary and winded to a combat with thirty
fresh enemies. The man they were chasing
was unarmed, and to deal with him such a
force was entirely unnecessary. Turning as he
ran, he cried out:

" Let the two swiftest follow me, and the
rest come slowly and spare themselves."

A moment later he saw that the order or
suggestion had been understood and practically
obeyed. Only three of the Karanians were
now close at his heels. The others had fallen
back and were following more leisurely.

For the leaders, however, there was no respite. It was Vance's nerve-force that was
setting the pace for his exhausted body and
refusing him even the knowledge that he was
tired. Still, he was not gaining ground, nor,

for that matter, was he losing it. Several
times he caught the glint of a naked brown
body bounding some distance ahead, but each
time ere he could raise his pistol to take aim
its mark was again covered by the low-hanging
foliage. Meanwhile he felt there could be
little distance left between them and the end
of the course, and then! — well, he could only
urge his muscles to renewed effort.

Suddenly the woods seemed to become
thinner, the clearing loomed up ahead, and
Vance saw the fleeing priest about ten strides
in advance running swiftly toward a group of
armed men with red tunics and black mantles
who were clustered before the house of Tao.
To stop short and raise his pistol was the work
of an instant. He covered his man and aimed
low and carefully. Then he fired, and a second
later had the satisfaction of seeing the fellow
pitch forward and roll on the ground almost at
the feet of the thirty guards who gazed dumbly
at the scene, but with more astonishment than
terror in their grim faces.

Vance had only time to dart back among the
trees and begin to load the empty chambers of

his revolver, when he heard the messenger, who, as misfortune would have it, had been only desperately wounded, screaming something in the island language to those gathered around him. At first they hesitated and looked wonderingly at each other, as if the information received was incredible; but a moment later one of the band identified the wounded man as a member of their own caste. They had not, however, recognised the pursuer, whose stained skin and dress, or what was left of it, had seemed, in the moment during which he had been visible, to mark him also for a priest. It was all incomprehensible to them and they feared some snare. A fresh torrent of words, gasped and groaned out by the dying Karanian, finally dispelled their doubts, and cries of grief and rage resounded through the forest. Several knelt beside the prostrate figure, some started toward the point where Vance had disappeared, while others drew back toward the house and eyed the winding stairway that ran up to the roof.

These last the American watched closely, fully realising that every instant of indecision on their part was vital to his success. Only three panting and exhausted men were with him,— a hopeless force with which to attack thirty guards, and the moments of delay served to bring his nine remaining followers nearer to the spot where the last decisive conflict must take place. Some such idea as this seemed also to come to the wounded priest, for he again screamed out several words, the effect of which upon his hearers was electric. Almost with one accord, they turned and hurried toward the stairway.

There was no room now for further inaction. Vance sprang from his cover and rushed forward, while his three tired companions followed, evidently prepared to stand by him bravely.

There were two courses that offered themselves: one, to try to cut their way through the crowd and gain and hold the ascent until the arrival of the rest of his men; the other, to stand back and pick off the priests, one by one, as they mounted to the roof. The former seemed absolutely hopeless, the latter nearly so. Realising this, he called out to his fellows

to halt, and two heard him and obeyed wonderingly. The third, now fighting mad, kept
right on and plunged among the black robes,
cutting and thrusting right and left until
he fell beneath a dozen wounds, after killing
one of the enemy and wounding a couple
more.

Meanwhile Vance had fired twice with deliberate aim, and each time the leader of the
line that had already commenced to ascend
the stairs rolled off to the ground. The two
nobles eyed his work with undisguised admira-
tion and, divining the purpose and wisdom of
his course, prepared quietly to defend him
against the ten or twelve men who now rushed
toward the spot whence this fiery destruction
issued. To these latter the American could
give no heed. The would-be murderers upon
the steps demanded all his attention.

One of his revolvers was now empty, but
only one of its shots had been wasted. He
thrust it mechanically into his belt and drew
the other. By this time both of his defenders
were down. Only three of their assailants had
fallen with them, and the survivors of the

latter sprang at him with their swords dripping blood.

He was conscious of a momentary hesitation
as to whether to fire in defence of himself or
to continue his practice upon those mounting
the house.   Then the stream of flame shot
from the levelled barrel, and another man
tumbled off the stairway.   As Vance drew one
short, quick breath in full expectation that the
brandished swords would make it his last, the
clash of weapons sounded in his ears and he
found himself wondering vaguely how he came
to be still alive.

The explanation was apparent, though.   The
rest of his followers had arrived and a surging
mass of fighting men writhed before him like
a tangle of huge serpents.   His eyes again
sought the stairway, and he started to see that
it was unoccupied.   Surely no one could have
gained the top!   As many as were still mounting must be now climbing that part of the
spiral that lay upon the other side of the house.

He had scarcely jumped to this conclusion
when its truth became evident.   A man's head
and shoulders rose above the roof, and then

an entire figure, but only to fall back at the
discharge of the revolver. Another and another fell. Vance's hand seemed as steady as
though it were a bar of iron. But one charge
remained now in the cylinder, and, as still another dark figure appeared and sprang toward
the centre platform, he levelled his weapon for
the last time and fired.

The fellow was undoubtedly hit, for he reeled
and staggered a moment and then either fell or
sprang down into the interior of the building.

Vance waited no longer. Dropping the empty
revolver upon the ground, he drew his sword
and darted toward the house of Tao, cutting
down a priest who attempted to bar his way.
The rest of his adversaries were too busily employed to notice, much less to stop him, but
one of his own men succeeded in disentangling
himself from the *mêlée* and followed. Gaining
the house, the American bounded up the winding stairs. In a moment he was upon the roof,
and then, without waiting to look, swung himself through the aperture and dropped to the
floor. He felt his exhausted legs yield under
him, and, as he tumbled in a heap, he was

vaguely conscious of a sword-point thrusting straight at his heart. Instinctively he threw up his hand and caught the descending arm. Grappling now with this last antagonist, he groped blindly for his own sword, which had fallen from his grasp, when suddenly a sharp cry of warning came from above. The mist seemed to pass from before his eyes, and he knew that it was Zelkah herself with whom he was struggling.

CHAPTER XXIII

BESIEGED IN TURN

GRADUALLY Vance's eyes accustomed themselves to the dim light. He saw the form of the priest he had last shot lying beside him stone-dead, and realised that the girl, mistaking himself in his disguise for another of her enemies, had endeavoured to defend herself against him with the sword of the first comer.

Even now it must have been far from easy to recognise in the battered and stained figure at her feet the stranger who had spoken the words she had been taught she must never hear, but, as the glow of recognition passed slowly across her face, paler somewhat than when Vance had seen it last, but with its perfect outlines unmarred, her slender form swayed slightly.

A man's strength must be very far spent
when such a situation does not arouse him to
a realisation of its demands, and Richard
Vance had not yet reached that state of exhaustion.   He managed to struggle to his feet
in time to catch Zelkah in his arms, now almost
fainting from the sudden revulsion of feeling,
and to crush her to his bosom with a strength
he would not have believed himself to possess.

" Why did you not obey me, my beloved ? "
she murmured; and even to Vance's jaded
faculties enough of reason remained for him to
know that kisses were the most appropriate
answer to such a very feminine interrogatory.
For a few moments he seemed to himself to
be wrapped in some wild dream inspired by
the black smoke of the East.   The gorgeous-
ness of his surroundings, the dark face of the
dead man at his feet, and the Oriental perfec-
tion of beauty in his arms, were like the phantasms of an Arabian Night.

But there was little time to surrender himself to the soft voluptuousness that threatened
to steal away his senses.   For a minute — and
probably all that had happened since his

entering the house of Tao had not occupied
more than that time — he had been entirely unconscious of the noises of the combat raging
without; and now he was first recalled to himself
by their sudden cessation.   Then he heard the
same voice that had so opportunely prevented
either himself or Zelkah from dying by the
hand of the other, and, glancing up to the circular orifice above, saw the bearded face of the
noble who had followed him to the roof.   The
man's words were simple and ominous.

"All our men are down and there are four
of the priests left.   I, Sirom, will defend the
stairway."

Vance saw at once the peril which still surrounded him, trapped as he was in a place
whence there was no possible chance of escape
and where he could do nothing but wait to be
released by a friend or have his throat cut by
an enemy.   He could hardly blame himself for
his descent, for he had been necessarily ignorant of the condition of the priest who had
dropped through the roof-entrance; but he
bitterly regretted that he had thrown away one
of his revolvers.   As it stood now, there was

nothing to do but to reload the one he still had, and, seating himself, with Zelkah at his feet, to listen to the struggle of his last ally to maintain his post.

As for the girl herself, no one could have been more oblivious that aught was occurring which could threaten their safety or joy. With hands clasped over his knee, she seemed to fix her long, liquid eyes on his like some beautiful and beneficent serpent seeking to charm away all thoughts that could interfere with perfect gladness. The attitude, the face, the nimbus of soul and sense and perfume that surrounded her would alone have proved the Karanians to be an Oriental race, had all other evidence been lacking.

And now the sounds of new combat waxed ominous. The prisoner could hear, first, the rush of feet up the stairway, then a momentary scuffle at some point of the circumference, followed by a short gasp and the thud of a body falling to the grass. Four times the same succession of noises was repeated, and not a word or shout had been uttered. A moment later the face of Sirom again appeared at the orifice.

" They are dead, my lord," he said quietly,
" and I am but little hurt.   A cut in the leg,
— that is all."

" Thank God!" cried Vance, in his native
tongue.   Then he continued in his jargon of
Hebrew, Phœnician, and Karanian, " And
now, if you can help us out of this hole, I will
attend to your wound, and ——"

" May Tao save us!" cried out Sirom, suddenly.   " Here are at least fifty priests escaped
from the square or the temple."

Again he withdrew from the opening.
Vance heard the hum of voices and the tread
of feet hurrying from the woods.   Then a
shout rose, doubtless as their eyes fell upon
Sirom, and almost immediately after came a
new rush up and around the stairway, followed
by the thud of falling bodies that told of a
well-maintained defence.

A few moments passed thus, and at last the
tide seemed to recede; but, before Vance
could wonder how Sirom had been able alone
to repulse so great a force, he heard a sharp
crack as of a small stone striking against
masonry, and then a shower of similar missiles
20

seemed to fall upon the roof. The next instant the orifice above was darkened and their champion swung himself through it and dropped to the floor. He was bleeding badly from a deep gash just below the knee, and his left arm hung helpless by his side.

"They are using their *baleri*," he said. "A stone broke my arm. It is impossible to hold the top any longer."

It flashed across Vance's mind even in this new emergency that by " baleri " the Karanian must mean slings and that the slingers of the Balearic Islands had been famous among the mercenaries who served Carthage; but such wandering thoughts were quickly dismissed and his brain bent to a contemplation of the danger that confronted them. In spite of it all, he found himself becoming calmer and more confident. The successful outcome of the train of seemingly unavertible perils through which his hopes had passed had given birth to a sort of fatalistic assurance that, threaten what might, the result must yet in some way be fortunate.

The time, however, for reflections of any kind was short, for before even an opportunity was afforded to examine Sirom's injuries there came again to their ears the sound of many feet circling the wall and gliding upward. They had scarcely drawn back to one side when a face peered through the aperture. Vance fired, and the head drooped and hung over with the blood dripping from it onto the floor below. Zelkah covered her eyes.

There was an instant's delay above, just time to allow Vance to reload the empty chamber of his revolver, and then the ghastly spectacle disappeared, as the body was drawn back to make room for another man, who now proceeded to swing himself over the edge with his hands. Another shot rang out before he had time to release his hold, and he came down in a writhing heap. Three more followed him in quick succession and fell as quickly.

The revolver was now empty and a pile of dead and dying men cumbered the floor in the middle of the room, while the smoke choked the lungs of the living and floated slowly up through its single outlet. But one of their besiegers had reached the bottom in a condition to be dangerous, and Sirom had managed to despatch him before he could gain his feet.

Then the attack was renewed, but from this on Vance was compelled to depend upon his sword and that of his injured companion. It was fortunate for them that the hole in the roof would not admit more than one enemy at a time. The drop, too, was sufficiently far to stagger a man, especially when he landed unexpectedly upon a writhing mass of human bodies, and, whether he slipped or staggered or fell, there was always a defenceless instant in which a well-directed blow or thrust served to bring him down. Then Sirom's sword soon rendered him harmless.

Still, even with these advantages, the contest could hardly be kept up forever. The assailants seemed absolutely reckless, the sword-arms of the garrison were fast becoming weary and their weapons dull, while the very corpses of their enemies promised soon to overwhelm them or at least to rise so high as to admit of the others stepping down instead of jumping.

But just at this point the attack stopped as suddenly as it had begun and Vance seized

the respite to drag some of the dead and
wounded to one side, so as to make room for
more.   Every moment gave breath to his lungs
and strength to his muscles.   He had again reloaded his revolver. A glance backward showed
him that Sirom had at last fainted from loss of
blood and that Zelkah was engaged in binding
up his wounds as well as she could with cloth
of gold gorgeously embroidered.   A deep
murmur as of many voices came to the ears of
the prisoners.

Still the renewal of the assault was delayed,
and now came the explanation of it all.   The
slingers' bullets began again to patter upon
the roof, the rush of footsteps again mounted
the stairs, the sound of falling bodies lent its
deadly import, while words of command rang
from the clearing and the woods beyond.
Evidently the ever-turning tables had been
turned yet again; the victorious Karanian
nobles had come up, and the late besiegers
were themselves besieged.

For Vance there was nothing to do but wait
until his final destiny should be fought out by
others, and, for once in his life, he yielded to

this usually most distressing of situations with something closely akin to relief. He distinguished three distinct assaults, each of which was evidently beaten back with considerable loss, while all the time the hail of stones fell steadily upon the roof. He found himself cursing the foolhardiness of assailants who persisted in storming a position practically defensible by a single man, but he forgot that they must be as uncertain as he had been of how prompt their help would have to be to prove available. After the third attack, however, the last comers seemed to become convinced of the futility of such efforts, for they drew back and bègan to depend entirely upon missiles. The stone bullets fell in showers and several of them, round and polished as grape-shot, whirled through the roof orifice and rebounded from the interior wall. The defence was manifestly weakening to the point of despair. Two more priests dropped, one after another, through the opening, to be as promptly shot as had been their predecessors. Then came another rush, a last brief struggle with defenders evidently all wounded and

exhausted unto death, and Vance's heart leaped
to see the pale, bearded face of a Carthaginian
looking wonderingly down at him and striving
to accustom his eyes to the smoke and darkness so as to distinguish the dead from the
living.

The next moment the American gave way to
the strain he had sustained so long, and
dropped, like a stone from a sling, upon the
reeking pavement.

All these events took place in January and
February of 1839; but not more than twenty
years have passed since a former officer of the
United States navy was ruling over a colony
of Carthaginian exiles upon an island indicated
on no extant map or chart.   It is barely possible that he may rule there to-day,— an old
man, but doubtless a happy one,— with her
who, sixty years ago, was the most beautiful
princess that the ancient blood of Phœnicia
ever warmed to life.

The priests of Tao died,— all save Lirrhi,—
and their bodies were dragged from square and
temple and cast into the bridal house of their

god, which was then buried under a great mound of earth, that they might moulder with the barbarous creed they served; while the once dreaded mountain pours its molten streams deep under the sea and troubles no longer the husbandman and the shepherd.

There were princes, too, of a new race in Karana twenty years ago,— tall men with dark eyes and brown, curling beards,—and princesses almost as beautiful as the one who made their father forget home and kin and rank for such kisses as colder climes and ages have frozen upon the lips of colder races than those that once enjoyed the earth.

THE END

www.ingramcontent.com/pod-product-compliance
Lightning Source LLC
Chambersburg PA
CBHW030244030726
47493CB00023B/582